"Usually my breakfast guests have spent the night, Lindsey."

He sidled up to her and pressed her between the concrete wall of the basement and the muscular wall of his chest. The musk of man and perspiration filled her senses. The cold of the concrete seeped through the back of her sweater while his heat scorched her front.

"If that had been the case," he continued, his voice dropping to a low and intimate level, "I'd make you the most incredible breakfast."

Lindsey shifted her gaze to his face, only inches from hers, and batted her lashes. "If I'd spent the night with you, Dylan, you wouldn't have the strength to make breakfast."

Dear Harlequin Intrigue Reader,

May holds more mayhem for you in this action-packed month of terrific titles.

Patricia Rosemoor revisits her popular series THE McKENNA LEGACY in this first of a two-book miniseries. Irishman Curran McKenna has a gift for gentling horses—and the ladies. But Thoroughbred horse owner Jane Grantham refuses to be tamed—especially when she is guarding not only her heart, but secrets that could turn deadly. Will she succumb to this *Mysterious Stranger*?

Bestselling author Joanna Wayne delivers the final book in our MORIAH'S LANDING in-line continuity series. In *Behind the Veil*, we finally meet the brooding recluse Dr. David Bryson. Haunted for years by his fiancée's death, he meets a new woman in town who wants to teach him how to love again. But when she is targeted as a killer's next victim, David will use any means necessary to make sure that history doesn't repeat itself.

The Bride and the Mercenary continues Harper Allen's suspenseful miniseries THE AVENGERS. For two years Ainslie O'Connor believed that the man she'd passionately loved—Seamus Malone—was dead. But then she arrives at her own society wedding, only to find that her dead lover is still alive! Will Seamus's memory return in time to save them both?

And finally, we are thrilled to introduce a brand-new author—Lisa Childs. You won't want to miss her very first book *Return of the Lawman*—with so many twists and turns, it will keep you guessing…and looking for more great stories from her!

Happy reading,

Denise O'Sullivan
Associate Senior Editor
Harlequin Intrigue

RETURN OF THE LAWMAN
LISA CHILDS

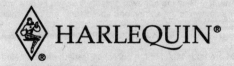

HARLEQUIN®

TORONTO • NEW YORK • LONDON
AMSTERDAM • PARIS • SYDNEY • HAMBURG
STOCKHOLM • ATHENS • TOKYO • MILAN • MADRID
PRAGUE • WARSAW • BUDAPEST • AUCKLAND

ISBN 0-373-22664-0

RETURN OF THE LAWMAN

ABOUT THE AUTHOR

Lisa Childs has been writing since she could first form sentences. At eleven she won her first writing award and was interviewed by the local newspaper. That story's plot revolved around a kidnapping, probably something she wished on any of her six siblings. A Halloween birthday predestined a life of writing Intrigue. She enjoys the mix of suspense and romance.

Readers can write to Lisa at P.O. Box 139, Marne, MI 49435, or visit her at her Web site www.lisachilds.com.

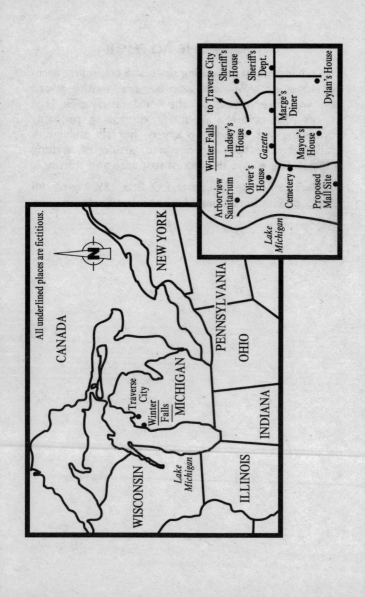

All underlined places are fictitious.

CANADA

NEW YORK

PENNSYLVANIA

OHIO

INDIANA

ILLINOIS

WISCONSIN

MICHIGAN

Traverse City

Winter Falls

Lake Michigan

to Traverse City

Sheriff's House

Sheriff's Dept.

Winter Falls

Lindsey's House

Gazette

Arborview Sanitarium

Oliver's House

Marge's Diner

Dylan's House

Mayor's House

Cemetery

Proposed Mall Site

Lake Michigan

CAST OF CHARACTERS

Dylan Matthews—After a decade, the detached lawman returns home to deal with the pain of his past.

Lindsey Warner—With a broken heart and a bruised ego the reporter returns to her rumor-filled hometown.

Sheriff Buck Adams—What secrets does the small-town sheriff keep that my cost his new deputy his life?

Chet Oliver—This retired lawyer believes in fighting a new development and keeping his secrets.

Mayor Reynolds—His fight to keep his town small may turn deadly.

William Warner—Lindsey's father has secrets he keeps for his daughter's safety.

Retha Warner—Lindsey's mother's madness is partly why Lindsey left home.

Sarah Hutchins—She's come home to settle old scores with the help of her wealthy husband.

Evan Quade—Is he a rich man's hired thug, or more?

Marge Zinser—The diner owner knows all the town's secrets.

Prologue

Through the sprinkling of white flakes on his windshield, Dylan Matthews noted the police cruiser parked in his driveway. The flashing lights cast a red-and-blue glow on the naked tree trunks lining the gravel drive.

His hand trembled as he jerked the shifter into Park and reached for the door handle. He'd heard the call on his radio. Disembodied voices tumbled out of the box on his dash. An ambulance was dispatched, but the sheriff told them it was too late. Jimmy was dead.

With a snap of his wrist he shut off the siren that wailed his arrival in his police cruiser. Dylan Matthews was a rookie deputy in the Winter Falls sheriff's office. He had to perform his official duties as a deputy. He'd already failed in his duty as a brother.

With a deep breath, he forced himself to find the detachment that had helped him through all the ordeals in his twenty-two years. He closed his eyes and tumbled ten years back to the searing pain of being trapped in a wrecked car. He could hear the echo of his own cries, and then his father's command. ''Shut it off, boy. Don't let the pain control you. Don't let yourself feel it.''

With another deep breath he forced down the panic and despair, locked it in a deep part of his soul with all the rest. He'd deal with it someday.

Dylan stepped out of the car onto the leaves littering the drive and crunched the calling cards of autumn beneath his boots. Snowflakes glittered on the russet leaves, another sign of Dylan's favorite season in northern Michigan.

He'd heard the crunch of leaves, but he barely noticed the screech of brakes as a Jeep jerked to a stop behind his car. Forcing himself out of his stupor, he turned to identify the new arrival.

Lindsey Warner. Over the last few months he'd forced himself to be detached about the teenage daughter of the editor of the *Winter Falls Gazette*. She was relentless in her pursuit of him, but either out of chivalry or self-preservation, he pretended not to notice.

But he noticed too much about her. Her glossy black curls. Her curvaceous body. Her sassy mouth. She was too young. But Jimmy had told him to take what she offered. Jimmy…

''I just heard it on my dad's scanner. It can't be true!'' The words burst from her mouth as she catapulted out of her vehicle.

He couldn't deal with Lindsey Warner right now and turned away from her.

He had to go inside the house. His duty as a police officer was to secure the crime scene. And he had to know if the call was correct. He had to see that his brother was dead before he could accept the horror of it. Again he fought down the despair.

His heart pounded against his ribs as he walked blindly past the sheriff's patrol car. He only made it a few more steps before she was at his side. She slipped her hand into his. Cold. Her fingers were cold, and her eyes were huge shadows in her face. She looked as horrified as he would feel if he allowed himself to feel anything.

"Deputy Matthews, Dylan, are you all right?"

Before he could answer, Sheriff Buck Adams joined them. "I'm so sorry, Dylan. Don't go inside. Let the girl take you someplace else. Anywhere else. I'll handle this for you."

But Dylan couldn't let someone else handle Jimmy. For so many years, even before their dad's death, he and Jimmy had faced the world alone. Could he face it without Jimmy?

He'd meant to drop her hand, but he still clutched her cold fingers in his. Only a few more feet lay between him and the back door. Somehow, on precariously shaking legs, he made it to the screen door of the kitchen. Through the old and snagged mesh, he saw Jimmy lying on the wooden floor in front of the half-open refrigerator. A bright red stain spread from beneath his body across the scratched maple boards.

Jimmy stared back at him. The wide blue eyes held no pain, only surprise. Was he surprised Dylan had let him down? He shouldn't have been. Dylan had never been able to save anyone he loved. As a lawman, he had been deputized to serve and protect. But he had not protected his brother from murder.

He dropped Lindsey Warner's hand. "Dylan, I'm so sorry," she said softly, or maybe it just sounded soft over the roaring in his ears. In the glare of the porch light, tears streaked from her dark eyes to her trembling chin.

He should have been the one to weep. But there was not even the threat of tears. In fact, his eyes were so dry they burned as if he'd spent a windy day on nearby Lake Michigan. "I'm sorry, too," he whispered. "You shouldn't have seen this." He gestured at the screen door.

"Dylan, you worry too much about everyone else. You calm down the old ladies who imagine stalkers are peeking in their windows. You try to slow down the reckless speeders for their safety."

"It's my job."

"But who takes care of you?" She reached for him again.

He took a quick step back. "Sheriff," he called out. "Please see she gets home safely. She shouldn't have been here."

Then he walked away from Lindsey Warner, from the crime scene, his home.... When he passed the sheriff's car, he glanced at the man in the back seat. Jimmy's best friend. Jimmy's killer.

His police instincts screamed at him. This wasn't right. But the sheriff had caught Steve Mars with the murder weapon in his hand. A knife from the block on the counter. For those two men it was over. For Dylan, the nightmare had just begun.

Chapter One

Ten years later...

With white knuckles wrapped around the leather-covered steering wheel, Dylan drove past the cemetery. Ancient oaks shed colored leaves onto perfectly groomed graves, but Dylan didn't slow to watch them fall.

He continued toward the heart of town, beyond the new hotels and motels and small strip malls to where the frame walls of the buildings were weathered and the brick was worn. He pulled into a parking lot behind an old Victorian house, which had been converted to a diner before Dylan was born.

For ten years he'd carried a picture of home in his head. And despite the nightmares, it was home. This small northern Michigan town had grown. Dylan had not expected that. He'd thought everything would remain the same, perhaps as a shrine to Jimmy.

Before he stepped from his black Expedition into the lot of the local diner, he slipped the shiny badge onto the pocket of his tan uniform. Winter Falls deputy. He didn't need to glance in the rearview mirror to witness the irony in his smile. His name and badge number were engraved below the title. Sheriff Buck had kept it for him.

For the last decade he'd hidden on the streets of Detroit. Rare had been the opportunity when he'd been able to carry the Detroit PD, Narcotics Division, badge. He'd been so deep undercover he'd thought he'd never come out. A few times he nearly hadn't.

The last scrape had forced Dylan to face some hard facts. His commanding officer had given him an ultimatum—either get some psychiatric help for his death wish or take some time off. Dylan had turned in that badge and decided it was time to come home.

Although he'd hoped to slip into the diner unseen, he'd forgotten the sharp eyes of the proprietress. "Dylan Matthews!" She launched herself into his arms.

Interested faces turned toward him. Only a few, like the mayor and his old fishing buddy, were familiar. The town had grown, but Marge's Diner was still the afternoon hub. "Marge, it's nice to see you." Awkwardly he reached down to pat her shoulder. Although she was petite, her grip was tight.

"It's been too long," she gasped when she finally released him. "You're home, then?"

He thought of the new businesses, the new faces, the old nightmares.... "Yeah." He tapped the badge. "I'm home."

A tinkling bell signaled another arrival. The sheriff slapped a hand on his shoulder. "Marge, get the boy something to eat. He looks half starved. Too skinny.

I told him to meet me here. I promised him he'd get a good meal from you, not a lecture.''

''I wasn't lecturing.'' She sniffed and dabbed at tears with the edge of her apron.

Sheriff Buck Adams wedged his girth into the vinyl booth that had been ''his'' as long as Dylan could remember. When Dylan had been a boy, he'd sat on a phone book to share a milk shake with his idol.

Now Marge set a mug of coffee before him. ''I'll get you a special, Dylan. You need some fuel. You look worn out. I can't believe the surprise. Both you and that little Lindsey Warner home from the big city. I thought we'd never see either of you again.''

The sip of hot coffee he'd taken scorched his throat as he choked ''Lindsey?'' Ten years had passed, but he could still picture her wild mane of midnight curls and her snapping ebony eyes. And her sassy mouth.

''She wasn't in Detroit, of course. She was in Chicago, working on some big newspaper when she got her heart broke. Should have stayed home and helped her daddy with the paper here, but I guess the *Winter Falls Gazette* wasn't good enough. She's back now, though, subdued I bet.''

Subdued? Lindsey Warner? He hoped not.

The sheriff waved Marge away. ''Don't get her started. She'll be sending out wedding announcements if you show any interest. Of course, you never did, but Lindsey wasn't so shy. That girl knew where your speed trap—''

''I thought we didn't call it that,'' Dylan teased the older man.

The sheriff waved his beefy hand again. ''Whatever we called it, she knew where it was. How many tickets you give that girl?''

''I don't remember.'' Five warnings. Five citations. She'd been reduced to a restricted license because of him.

''Yeah, she was too young. What, sixteen?''

Sweet sixteen. And how he wished he'd kissed her.

''And you were what? Twenty-one?''

''Twenty-two when I left,'' Dylan reminded him. But in his soul, so much older than those years.

''That was a heck of a mess, Dylan. I knew you didn't have anything to do with that boy's suicide. I should've searched him when he got back from sentencing. But after killing Jimmy, the guilt got Steve Mars to hang himself in jail, not you. There's just a bunch of busybodies in this town with nothing better to talk about.'' Sheriff Buck's face reddened, and a vein jumped at his temple. ''I should've—''

''You stuck by me, Sheriff. You always have,'' Dylan assured him, and closed his eyes. Behind his lids flashed a memory from when he was twelve, and the sheriff had rescued him from the car accident that had left him motherless. ''You always were...''

''I'm glad you're home, boy. I need you around here. It's not so quiet anymore. More to worry about now than some lovesick teenage girl speeding around town.''

Dylan nodded, but disappointment rose in his throat. After all those years of senseless violence in Detroit, he'd wanted to return home where but for that one night, he'd had nothing more dangerous to worry about than a sassy teenager.

"Lindsey Warner subdued?" he muttered.

The sheriff chortled. "Don't show any interest," he hissed as Marge slapped some steaming plates of beefy noodle casserole on the table.

"I haven't had a casserole in years, Marge. Thanks." Dylan reached for the fork. He hoped he could eat. Too many memories had his guts tied in knots.

She patted his head the way she had when he was eight years old. He had to smile. Nobody had patted his head in ten years. It was good to be home.

IT WAS HELL TO BE HOME, Lindsey thought as she leaned back in her father's chair. Throughout the office a satisfying bang echoed as she swung the heels of her boots onto the surface of his old desk. She would have rather kicked something, though.

"Hey, brat," her father teased as he poked his graying head around the door. "Taking over already? Or hiding out?"

She glared at him, her most lethal glare. He laughed. Then he lifted a bag and waved it in the air in mockery of a flag of surrender. The sweet memory of Marge's Diner drifted across the room to her. The smell of cinnamon rolls and strong coffee cut across the stale air of old cigars and newsprint that always prevailed in her father's office.

She'd missed the stale odor. She'd missed the cinnamon rolls and coffee, too. "If that's what I think it is, I'll let you stay on for a while before I put you in a retirement home, old man." But she'd missed her father most.

She swung her boots from his desk and jumped up, but he waved her back down and took the chair across from her. "Get used to it, honey. It will be yours one day."

"I don't deserve it, Dad," she said softly as she took the grease-stained bag from his hands and spread the decadent bounty across his already cluttered desk.

"It's better than not wanting it." He expelled a weary-sounding sigh. Lindsey's gaze clung to his gently wrinkling face. She'd been gone too long. Although he'd come to Chicago for visits, the time had been too brief and passed quickly. He'd aged, and Lindsey hadn't been able to witness every new line in his face, every new gray hair on his head.

"I never said I didn't want it," she reminded him.

"You just wanted more."

She winced over the hurt pride in his voice. "It's not that it wasn't enough. It's not mine. I wanted something for me. And I wanted out of this town!" With barely controlled anger she ripped off a sticky piece of roll.

"You ever going to forgive them?" he asked in the understanding tone that had always been her undoing.

She was too old for tears. "It's over. There are bigger hurts in this world."

He slid his rough hand over hers, and she turned hers over to link their fingers. "I hate that you had to find that out from a loser like your ex-fiancé."

"That's history now, Dad." She kicked her purse that leaned against her dad's desk. "He wouldn't take his ring back in person, so I'm going to mail it."

Her dad chuckled. "Pawn it. After the way he treated you…"

She squeezed his hand and forced a smile. "Yeah, well, that's why I had to leave, to get used and abused in the big city." The smile threatened to slip. "I can appreciate Winter Falls now."

"Can you?" her father taunted knowingly.

She laughed. "All right. Not yet. But I will if I decide to stay. I haven't decided yet, Dad."

"It's not the same town, brat. There's so much growth. New shops, new commerce. Snowmobilers in the winter. Boaters in the spring and summer, and hunters in the fall. A wealthy developer wants to build a huge mall on an old farm just east of town. Winter Falls is in the process of a major growth spurt."

His excitement spilled over in his voice, and Lindsey tried to summon some of her own. But she was more excited over the richness of the sticky cinnamon roll and the bite of the bitter, hot coffee.

Her father laughed. "But you need more action. You were reporting the police beat too long."

"I wasn't covering it alone, just assisting." She winced over the bitterness in her voice, and her pride stung all over again with her stupidity. Why had she accepted her ex-fiancé's lies?

"I read the paper, honey. I recognize my daughter's voice whether I hear it over the phone or read it in newsprint."

She took another gulp of coffee and enjoyed the numbness following the burn. She'd been numb for a while now. It was better that way. "Any action here?"

"Heated debates over the mall proposal. An old trustee and the mayor are fighting it. The developer is rich and powerful. It's interesting. It's not life and death, but it's interesting."

She sighed. "You're right. It is interesting. I don't need life and death anymore. Well, not death, anyhow."

Her father opened his mouth, but if he scrambled for words, none came out. He stuffed a piece of roll between his lips. They ate in silence for several moments before he spoke again.

Finally he asked, "Are you going to see her, Lindsey?"

She didn't need to ask of whom he spoke. "Would it matter? Would she even know?" She popped another piece of roll into her mouth, but it was like chewing sawdust now.

"I'll be honest with you, honey. She probably wouldn't know you. But I think it might matter to you." He reached for her hand again, but she pulled back and wrapped it around her cup of coffee.

None of the warmth permeated her icy cold fingers. "I'll be honest with you, Dad. I don't think it would."

He nodded, and disappointment flashed in his eyes. "On another note, there's more news...."

Lindsey leaned forward, recognizing the tone of her father's voice. This was something that would matter to her. "Yeah?"

"He's back."

"Who?"

"I wasn't going to tell you because I didn't want

you smashing out the taillight on your Jeep or any other foolishness...."

Lindsey's face heated, and she managed a giggle. She thought she'd lost the youthful ability to giggle. "Dylan Matthews?" Then she remembered how he had left ten years ago, and whatever pleasure she'd flirted with faded away. "I'm not the only one who has to forgive this town."

"According to Marge, he's sworn to protect it. He must have forgiven it."

She snorted. "I always wondered why you never hired Marge. She'd make a great reporter. She always scoops you." Her father's face reddened. Marge had an inside track with Will Warner despite his marriage.

And she remembered another reason why she'd left. Her father was part of this town with its gossip and secrets.

AFTERNOON HAD SLIPPED into evening. Dylan had spent it familiarizing himself with a town he'd once known so well. He'd spent it doing anything but returning to the scene of so many of his nightmares.

The leaves crunched under his feet as he walked around the Expedition and headed toward the abandoned house. In the fading light he barely noted the peeling paint and dirty windows. If he were ever fanciful, he might think it looked lonely. But that wasn't new. It had been lonely for a long time, ever since his mother had died.

Sheriff Buck had offered him a bed in his home, but part of Dylan's reason for returning to Winter Falls had been to deal with the house.

In northern Michigan fall had a nasty habit of slipping swiftly into winter. Dylan had originally planned a brief trip to Winter Falls to prepare the house for cold weather. The pipes needed to be drained and the water shut off.

And he could have easily asked the sheriff to handle it for him as he had in all the years past. But he hadn't asked because he'd realized how badly he wanted to leave Detroit for home. This was home. Even with all its nightmares.

He pulled open the screen door and slipped his key into the lock of the back door. It hadn't been locked or closed that night ten years ago. On rusty hinges the door creaked open.

Immediately he glanced at the spot in front of the refrigerator. The door of the old appliance was propped open, much as it had gaped that night. The maple boards had been stripped and revarnished, but still the stain shone through the gleaming surface.

Although his knees shook, Dylan forced himself across the floor. He dropped the house keys onto the counter, rubbed a hand over his face and wiped away beads of sweat.

The sheriff was right. He should have sold the house. Maybe it was that simple. He shouldn't have left town, just the house.

He reached into his pocket for a handkerchief and pulled out a letter. He'd received it before he'd left Detroit. He uncrumpled the paper and perused the shaky handwriting of an old man.

The Winter Falls postmark hadn't surprised Dylan. Sheriff Buck often wrote to him, and as he'd been working out his notice in Detroit, he had figured the sheriff had had details of Dylan's reemployment as a Winter Falls deputy.

Instead he'd found the letter had been written by the lawyer of the man who'd killed his brother and then later himself.

Although he hardly glanced at the words, Dylan recited them from memory.

Dylan,

As I hear you're returning home, I need to make an appointment with you to handle some unfinished business from ten years ago. I have something from Steve Mars that is addressed to you. I should have given it to you years ago, but when you left town, I thought you wanted to leave those painful memories behind. Now that you are returning, I feel it is my duty to deliver this item to you even though I am retired from my law practice. Please notify me when you return to town.

Sincerely,
Chet Oliver

Dylan crumpled the letter again and stuffed it back in the pocket of his leather jacket. Of the darkened room he asked, "Do I really want anything from Steve Mars?" His gaze fell on the stain on the hardwood floor. Others shadows blended into it, but he knew precisely where the stain began and ended.

Before he could give it any more thought, his cell

phone rang. He pulled it from his pocket and flipped it open. "Dylan Matthews."

"Deputy," the sheriff reminded him, but there was no teasing note in his voice. His booming voice shook.

"What's wrong, Sheriff?"

"Get over to Sunset Lane, Oliver's place. Something happened. I'm going to call it in, but I want you here first. Better yet, you call it in when you get here."

Dylan reached into his pocket and touched the letter. He remembered where Chet Oliver lived. He'd gone to the lawyer's house after Steve Mars's jail-cell suicide. He'd wanted to know if the lawyer had really believed Steve had killed Jimmy. Why hadn't the old man given him whatever Steve Mars had left for him then? Why keep it ten years?

Dylan slipped his phone into his pocket with the letter and picked up his keys. Would he finally get some answers tonight or only more questions?

WHILE HER FATHER WORKED on his editorial, Lindsey loomed over his shoulder, reading as he wrote. "You're brilliant, Dad. The things you notice…well, let's just say you're a much better reporter than many I've known."

Her father squeezed the hand she'd braced on his shoulder. "Brat."

Behind her on the scarred credenza, her father's police scanner sputtered out a call. Despite the static and the poor reception of the ancient model, she recognized the voice. Dylan Matthews. Deputy Dylan Matthews calling for the coroner.

"Chet?" her father gasped when the address sputtered out of the box.

"Chet Oliver. The lawyer? If he died of natural causes, why wouldn't they have called his family doctor?" Lindsey narrowed her eyes. Then she grabbed her backpack-style leather bag and slung it over her shoulder.

"Lindsey." Her father reached for her arm. "You're not going—"

"Do you want the story, Dad?"

Her father leaned back in his chair and stared at her over the rims of his reading glasses. "I want the story. Are you working for me?"

She'd come home to see her father. She'd not thought beyond that. "I guess I am."

"Then remember I'm the boss. Go easy on Dylan, okay, brat." He softened the warning with a smile.

"You want the story, Dad. To get it, I have to go to the story." And the man. Not that she wanted the man. She hadn't wanted him in a long time. She was over her adolescent crush.

In Chicago she'd learned it was better when wishes didn't come true. Idols were safer admired from afar. Up close they were human and flawed. When she saw Dylan Matthews again, she believed she'd see just the man, not a heart-stopping hero.

Chapter Two

Dylan snapped on his plastic gloves and touched the desk where Chet Oliver was slumped. A bullet in his temple. Dylan had already called the coroner, taken crime-scene photos and dusted for prints.

This was his inspection. The one that gave him a "feel" for what had happened that night. He hoped the crime scene would speak to him, not that he had much experience with murder investigations.

"It doesn't make any sense," Sheriff Buck muttered from the chair Dylan had pressed him into earlier. The tiny Queen Anne dubiously supported the sheriff's weight.

Oliver's Victorian farmhouse showcased several antiques. Dylan admired the gleaming mahogany surface of the desk as his fingertips skimmed over it.

He raised a white residue to eye level. Then he glanced up. Plaster from the ornate ceiling above Chet's desk. He spied a bullet hole near some cove molding.

"Did you find it?" Sheriff Buck asked, his breathing ragged.

Dylan glanced at him and wondered if he should

call the rookie deputy to look after the sheriff instead of having him wait outside for the coroner.

But the kid had turned green when he'd seen the victim, and Dylan had wanted him to get some air. Perhaps the sheriff needed some, too.

"What? A suicide note?" Dylan gestured at the retired lawyer's slumped body. "This was no suicide."

The sheriff sighed. "It wouldn't make sense for him to kill himself. He just retired. We went fishing a couple weeks ago. He was looking forward to retirement, to his fight with the developers...."

"Fight?"

"Over the proposed mall project. Chet is—was a trustee."

"You told me about the developer this afternoon." Dylan retraced his steps across the room. He dropped his hand on the sheriff's shoulder. "Oliver didn't do this."

"I saw the gun in his hand."

Dylan shook his head. "It was put there. A round was squeezed off. Red marks indicate there will be bruising on his hand. This is murder."

"It doesn't make sense...."

"How did you happen to find him, Sheriff? It's getting late for a visit."

The sheriff's shoulder trembled beneath Dylan's hand. "You didn't find it?"

"What? I already said there was no note—"

"Not from Oliver. It would have been from Steve Mars."

Dylan fought a shudder. A ghost hadn't killed Chet Oliver. "What are you talking about?"

"I'm talking about whatever Chet had for you. He came into the diner after you left today. He said he had something for you, something Steve Mars had wanted you to have."

Dylan nodded. "He sent a letter to me in Detroit. Told me the same thing."

"A letter's one thing. But the fool was talking about it in the middle of Marge's Diner. William Warner was there, getting something to go. It'll probably be all over tomorrow's paper. And for what? It's old news." The sheriff's face reddened, and his breathing grew more labored.

From an antique bureau, Dylan grabbed the glass of water he'd given him earlier and pressed it back into his hand. "Take a sip. Don't worry. It's all right."

"No, it's not. I came here to tell him to keep whatever it was. You didn't need to go through any of that pain again. You just came home. I didn't want him driving you away." The sheriff laid his hand over Dylan's.

Dylan glanced over his shoulder at the lifeless body of Chet Oliver. "He won't be doing that now. I looked through his desk and his filing cabinet. There wasn't anything addressed to me."

"That's just as well." The sheriff took a swallow of water.

Dylan shook his head. "But I wanted to know what Steve Mars had left for me. I need some answers. It's been ten years."

"Answers to what?" With a shaky hand, Sheriff Buck set his glass back on the bureau, sloshing water onto the gleaming wood. "Sometimes things just happen. There's no reason, no explanation. You just have to move on."

Dylan nodded as if he understood. But he didn't. He'd been gone ten years, but he'd never moved on. And for his part, neither had Sheriff Buck Adams.

After Dylan's mother had dumped him for Dylan's father, the sheriff had never married. He'd stayed in love with a married woman and then with a dead woman. No, the sheriff didn't know any more about moving on than Dylan did.

The young officer scrambled inside. His face flushed and eyes wide, he whispered, "She's out there."

Dylan narrowed his eyes. "Who?"

"A big-city reporter. She wants to talk to the officer in charge. She has questions, lots of them."

Lindsey Warner. "I didn't realize she was working for her father. I thought she was home—what had Marge said?"

The sheriff offered no information. The older man rested his head in his trembling hands.

"Yeah," Dylan continued as if he'd been given an answer, "with a broken heart. Subdued."

"Subdued!" The kid's voice cracked.

"She's not subdued?"

"Hell, no!" His face reddened even more. "Sorry, sir."

"You can handle her."

"No, sir, really you should talk to her. I've never talked to a reporter before."

"Tell her she can come to the station tomorrow. We'll have more information after the coroner gets here. We can't tell her anything tonight."

The young officer's eyes filled with doubt.

"You can do it—" Dylan read the badge pinned askew on the kid's shirt pocket "—Deputy Jones."

After the kid dragged his feet out the front door, Dylan squeezed the sheriff's shoulder again. "We'll get to the bottom of this. I promise. We'll find out who did this and why."

Murder had revisited Winter Falls. This time Dylan was going to get all the answers.

He thought again of the stain on his kitchen floor. He reined his thoughts in. Jimmy was gone. A new victim had taken his place. Dylan had to think of something else.

He thought of Lindsey Warner. Subdued. Hell, no.

"Suicide." Lindsey snorted at her reflection in the rearview mirror of her Jeep. Then she squinted against the glare of the morning sun ricocheting off the rusted hood.

The young deputy, Jones, had called it suicide. Of course, he hadn't offered it freely. No, Lindsey had had to pry the information from him.

Deputy Matthews had been stupid to let a rookie try to handle her. Even experienced, cynical city detectives hadn't been able to handle her.

She gripped the steering wheel tighter as the old

Jeep bounced along the gravel road. She was headed to the police department this morning, all right.

But after Jones's stuttered explanations, she hadn't returned home. Although she'd been gone awhile, she still had connections in this town. The coroner played cards with her father.

Despite the late hour, he'd given her an off-the-cuff preliminary report.

Murder. A murder in Winter Falls. Again.

How did Deputy Dylan Matthews feel about a murder on his first day back on the job?

She hadn't known Chet Oliver. She'd been gone nine years, and before then, she hadn't had need of lawyers or city trustees. Dylan knew him, though. Chet Oliver had represented his brother's murderer, but there hadn't been much to represent. Steve Mars had pleaded guilty. That case was closed.

Would this case be closed so easily? Although she hadn't known Oliver, she believed he hadn't deserved to die. Neither had Jimmy Matthews. She couldn't imagine how his brother's murder must still affect Dylan.

Sometimes it still affected her. His had been the first dead body she'd ever seen. Since then, on the police beat, she'd seen many more. It never got easier.

She shuddered and turned up the heat. Warm autumn mornings didn't exist in northern Michigan.

She pressed on the accelerator. She had some questions for Deputy Dylan Matthews. Over the clatter of the heater motor, a siren wailed. A glance in her rearview mirror confirmed the flashing lights on the vehicle behind her.

The Jeep tossed up a shower of stones as she ground it to a stop. The last thing she needed was another ticket. Her insurance premiums were putting the agent's kid through an Ivy League college as it was.

Then again, if it was young Deputy Jones, she would demonstrate to him how ill advised it was to lie to Lindsey Warner. Lindsey couldn't stand being lied to. Too many people already had.

But the long, muscular body that unwound from the police car was too honed to be the rookie's. Ten years had brought Dylan Matthews to his full, masculine potential. Despite how mad she was, Lindsey had to appreciate his long legs, lean hips and wide chest. His tan uniform displayed his impressive physique to perfection.

The brisk morning breeze tousled his golden blond hair. The sun glinted off the dark glasses he wore. She wanted them off. She wanted to see if his eyes were as deep a blue as she'd remembered in some stray dreams.

While she drooled over him, lost in la-la land, he tapped on the window. Startled, she quickly rolled it down.

"License and registration, ma'am." Deputy Dylan Matthews used the same deep, impersonal tone he'd always used when citing her for a traffic violation.

But then he'd used her name, at least. Was it possible he didn't recognize her? Was her father lying when he swore she had never changed a bit?

"How fast was I going, Officer?" she queried politely as she reached into her leather bag. Her fingers touched on her can of Mace, but she passed over it for her wallet.

"Fifteen over the posted speed limit" was his clipped reply. With a leather-gloved hand he accepted the license she'd pulled from its plastic sheath.

Because of the concealing dark glasses, she couldn't discern if he recognized the name. "Out-of-state license and plates," he observed. "I need to see your registration, too, please."

"What? You think I stole this car? This old thing? This is the same Jeep I drove when you pulled me over when I was a kid, Dylan Matthews!" She threw open the door and flew out of the vehicle.

He stepped back, but she was in his face with one stride. She reached for his dark glasses, but before she could whip them off, her wrist was caught tight in his leather-gloved hand.

"Ma'am, are you assaulting an officer?" he queried, his tone too nonchalant.

"Not yet."

"Are you going to invite me to frisk you like old times, Lindsey?" A grin teased one corner of his hard mouth.

She tried to pull her wrist free, but his grip was too tight. "Very funny, Dylan. You knew me the whole time!" She lifted her other hand to pry his fingers loose. He caught that one in the glove still holding her license. The hard plastic bit into her wrist. And he pulled her closer.

"Ooh." She feigned a sigh. "Getting physical with me, Deputy?"

"Isn't that what you were always tempting me to

do ten years ago, Lindsey?'' His voice had dropped to a low rumble in his chest, which vibrated against hers.

She took a quick breath. ''Were you ever tempted, Dylan?'' She hated the vulnerability that had slipped into her equally low voice. But he had been the first to break her foolish heart.

After a moment he offered, ''You were just a kid then.''

''That doesn't answer my question. Were you ever tempted to catch me any of those hundred times I threw myself at you?'' Her heart ached with the old pain of every one of his rejections.

He chuckled. ''Another woman would either deny throwing herself at a man, or, at the very least, never bring it up. There's no humility in you.'' He chuckled again and eased his grip on her wrists.

Despite her anger at him, for which he'd pay later, Lindsey was tempted to give in to desire. She leaned into his hard chest, his badge biting through her fleece pullover.

''Lindsey.'' Her name was a sexy rumble in his chest. Perhaps he'd meant it as a threat.

''Dylan.''

''Haven't learned to slow down yet?'' He clicked his tongue. ''How many times have I warned you about going too fast?''

''I like fast.''

His chuckle ended in a strained cough.

''You're not trying to bribe your way out of this ticket?'' He cleared his throat. ''You know it's a crime to bribe an officer.''

"What do you think I'm offering?" Lindsey asked with a coy flutter of her lashes.

Dylan shook his head. "I don't know. That's what scares me."

Lindsey batted her lashes again. "Aw, Deputy, it won't be anything you don't deserve." She flashed a bright smile.

Despite the dark lenses of his sunglasses, she read his reaction; he stiffened against her. His chiseled lips descended toward hers. In those dark lenses were twin reflections of herself, soft and feminine, yielding. Lindsey jerked back. The last thing she ever wanted to be again was yielding.

"Lindsey?" His head dipped close to hers, his lips just a breath away from hers. She could almost taste him.

"I want something, Dylan."

A dark blond brow lifted above the rim of the sunglasses.

"I want the truth." Although she leaned against him, she wasn't vulnerable anymore. She'd remembered her anger. She really hated being lied to, and her battered pride stung.

"Jeez, you are determined. Yes, damn it, I was tempted ten years ago. I was tempted to do this...." He dropped her wrists to pull her fully into his arms. Then one gloved hand grasped the back of her head and pulled her mouth to his.

She dodged away, so that his lips grazed her cheek. "That's not the truth I wanted, Dylan." But the fast pounding of her heart told another story.

He raised his head, and she fervently wished she

could see his eyes. His nostrils flared as he exhaled a deep breath. "What truth do you want, Lindsey?"

"Why are you trying to pass a murder off as a suicide?"

"What?" He dropped his arms from around her and stepped back.

She shivered from the loss of his body heat. "Why are you calling a murder a suicide?"

His response came softly but succinctly. "I didn't call anything a suicide."

"No, you didn't." She narrowed her eyes. "You sent your flunky to do your dirty work, to deal with the press."

He had the audacity to laugh. She wanted to belt him, but she suspected he'd arrest her for assaulting an officer. With an effort she grappled for control, amazed she'd almost lost it.

"So you're not denying it?"

"Denying what? I didn't send my flunky to do anything. I don't have a flunky. I told a young deputy to tell you to come by the station today, that we'd have more information then. Nothing was said about suicide. The deputy must have drawn his own conclusion. But none of that matters."

"No." A heavy sigh followed her agreement. "It doesn't. A man is dead, murdered, and you lied about it."

He chuckled again, but she shivered over the coldness in his tone. "You don't give up, Lindsey. I didn't lie about anything. You're trying to twist my words. Now I have some questions."

Imitating his gesture she raised a brow.

"I thought you just came home for a visit?" His voice dropped. "There was something about a broken heart?" He brushed the back of his knuckles over her cheek.

Heat climbed into her face, so she dipped her chin. "I guess the rumor mill is still as active as ever. I came home because I wanted to, not because I'm hiding or licking any wounds." She lifted her chin.

"So why are you covering this story?"

She'd flown out of her father's office the previous evening on the scent of a story. She hadn't thought beyond it. Was there any reason for her to stay in Winter Falls? Was there any reason for her to return to Chicago?

"Because there's a story."

He nodded. "And your father can't cover it on his own?"

She really needed to belt him. "No, my father isn't used to covering murder, Deputy."

"And you are?"

"I assisted on the police beat in Chicago. Yeah, I'm used to it. So you're admitting Chet Oliver was murdered?"

"No, you're saying that, Lindsey Warner, which makes me wonder how you would come to that conclusion if Jones told you suicide. What information or evidence has led you to believe this and how did you come by this evidence? You wouldn't have intruded on a crime scene? As a reporter who has covered a police beat, you would know better than that. You would know better than to possibly contaminate evidence."

She glared at him.

"Yeah, I would. I would never contaminate evidence. I've been gone awhile, but a good reporter has sources everywhere." She waited a full second while she carefully studied his handsome face. He wasn't giving. Neither was she.

After taking a hopefully calming breath, she asked, "Are you going to give the public the truth?"

"You're the public now, Lindsey?"

"Damn it, Dylan!"

"After I get the coroner's report, I'll give you more details. Anything I said before then would merely be speculation."

She couldn't curb her mocking smile.

"He's your source? You've already got the coroner's report or an idea of what will be on it." He sighed.

"A reporter protects her sources."

Behind his dark lenses, she sensed he carefully studied her. What did he speculate about her return to Winter Falls? Did he believe the rumor mill?

Before she could ask, a call sputtered from his police radio. Without a goodbye, he strode back to his cruiser.

He still had her license and wasn't above writing her up a citation. Because she was curious about the police call, she followed him.

She recognized the code for a missing person. Then Sheriff Buck spoke clearly. Her father often laughed about the sheriff not bothering with the codes. "Mrs. Warner has run away from the sanatorium. She's been missing since yesterday afternoon, Dylan. After searching the grounds and the surrounding area, the sanatorium finally contacted Warner, and he's been searching all night.''

Lindsey's heart clutched with fear. Her mother. Her poor, deranged mother had wandered off and spent the cold autumn evening outside. She sprinted toward her Jeep but didn't manage three steps before Dylan caught her arm.

"Lindsey, you can't drive away without your license.''

"Watch me!''

"Come on. Come with me. We'll find her.''

She listened for the pity the town had always drowned her in. She didn't hear it. But then Dylan's life was more deserving of pity than hers.

He directed her to the passenger side of the police car and opened the door for her. Before she could be touched by his gesture, she realized he regularly opened doors for people in police cars. Usually the people were criminals.

When he slid behind the wheel, he turned to her. Finally he removed the dark glasses. His blue eyes were as dazzling as they'd been in her dreams. Now, instead of pity, they were filled with concern. "Where would she be, Lindsey?''

Lindsey sighed. "I haven't seen her in nine years, Dylan.'' The guilt clogged her throat. "I know that sounds awful. You probably think I'm a selfish brat. But I couldn't…'' Her heart hadn't been able to handle any more of her mother's rejections. Before Lindsey had left for college, Retha Warner hadn't even recognized her only child.

He took her hand in his and gently squeezed her fingers. The last time they'd held hands had been after a murder.

"Okay." She dragged in a jerky breath and fought the urge to put her head between her knees. Panic danced through her stomach. "Okay. She would go home. Wouldn't she go home? God, would she remember where it is? She hasn't been there in almost ten years."

"I didn't know your mother was in a sanatorium."

"But you knew she was nuts. Everybody knows she's nuts. After she tried to kill herself, Dad had to put her in that place. She was a danger to herself. He had to." She winced over the defensive tone. The guilt danced with the panic. "You don't care about that." She dragged in another breath and hoped she wouldn't hyperventilate.

"Yes, I do, Lindsey."

She shrugged and then shivered. "Let's go home first. Maybe she'd get there. The last few years before I left, she didn't know me half the time, but maybe she'd remember how to get home."

Dylan squeezed her fingers again. "I know where your house is. And if she's not there, we'll keep looking. We'll find her."

She appreciated his calm assurance. Lindsey had never been good at serenity. While in the throes of her deep depression, her mother had always appeared too serene. She'd sit for days without moving, or even blinking, Lindsey had suspected.

"It's not the same." Dylan pulled into her father's driveway and turned off the ignition of the patrol car.

Lindsey glanced at the vinyl-sided Dutch colonial. "Not since you left, no. She set it on fire. She was inside." She hated the sting of tears behind her eyelids. That had been so long ago. She shouldn't still be able to smell the smoke in the air. She shouldn't remember the struggle for breath when she'd fought the heat and flames for her mother.

"I'm sorry." Dylan trailed a finger from his free hand down her cheek.

Lindsey let out a shuddery breath. "Why? You weren't here."

"That's why."

Despite not wanting him to see the tears swimming in her eyes, she turned toward him. He was so strong, so solid. "You're not responsible for me, Dylan. You had good reasons for leaving."

He didn't respond, but he didn't release her fingers, either. He hadn't even while he'd driven over the rutted country roads.

"She's not here, you know." Lindsey couldn't imagine where her mother would be. To get here from the sanatorium, she'd have had to walk miles. Did she have a jacket to keep her warm? Where had she slept? Lying in some rotted leaves in a ditch on the side of the road? Had they passed her?

Lindsey fought down the panic. "Her doctors think she might be schizophrenic, but her erratic symptoms have made her hard to diagnose. She wouldn't have recognized the old house, let alone the rebuilt one."

"But it's at the same address. We should check."

"I just left here a little while ago, on my way to see you at the police station."

He opened his door. "You can stay here. I'll check. Give me your keys."

"I left them in the Jeep."

He chuckled. "Well, I suppose it's safe. I doubt anyone will steal it."

She rewarded his obvious effort with a weak smile. "I'm sure Dad stashes the spare in the same place." She hopped out and strode to the door. They'd take a quick gander inside and resume their search. Retha Warner wasn't there. But they would find her. They had to.

Before Lindsey could reach above the door frame for the key, the kitchen door opened. A fragile-looking woman with dull black hair and glassy eyes reached for Lindsey. "Sweetheart, there you are! I couldn't catch you when you left the house for school earlier. Are you skipping class?" The woman made a tsking noise.

As she stood stiffly in the fragile arms of her mother, Lindsey trembled, and her stomach pitched as a flurry of emotions surged through her.

Her mother. She pushed some of the scraggly hair from her mother's scarred cheek. How did she recognize Lindsey now after all these years when she hadn't then, when a teenage girl had so desperately needed her mother?

"Deputy Matthews," Retha Warner said in a welcoming voice. "Thank you for bringing her home. She causing you trouble again?" She actually winked at him.

How had her mother known of Lindsey's infatuation with the young deputy? She'd always seemed oblivious to her surroundings.

"Mom," she finally said, struggling to clear her throat of the jerky sobs threatening as memories flooded her mind. "Mom, I'm not in school anymore. I'm almost twenty-seven now."

"Always trying to rush things, Lindsey," her mother scoffed affectionately. "Come in, you two. I've baked cookies and started coffee."

Dylan's hand on her back urged Lindsey inside the warm kitchen. Cookies cooled on waxed paper on the counter, and an announcer chattered from the radio on top of the refrigerator.

"Mom, please." She followed Retha to the counter and put a trembling hand on her shoulder. "You must know that you don't live here anymore."

"I know the house looks different. Remodeled, finally. I love it." Her mother smiled as she poured them mugs of steaming coffee.

Lindsey took her mother's hands in hers, running her fingers over the scarred flesh of the right one. She squeezed her eyes shut and struggled for a breath. Her mother hadn't even cried over the burns. But Lindsey had.

Dylan rubbed her back. "Let me tell her, Lindsey."

She shook her head and opened her eyes. Her mother's once beautiful face held concern and confusion. Lindsey dragged in a quick, choking breath. "Mom, you live in the sanatorium now."

"What? There is no sanatorium in Winter Falls." A frown puckered Retha's otherwise unlined forehead. She pulled her hands from Lindsey's.

Lindsey brushed the hair away from her mother's face. The thin strands of black slid smoothly between Lindsey's fingers. At least they kept her clean at the sanatorium even though they'd not kept her safe.

Lindsey took in another breath and caught the scent of roses. Her mother's perfumed soap clung to her.

"Arborview, Mom."

Her mother shuddered now. "Arborview is the home for unwed mothers, Lindsey. You shouldn't know anything about that place." She slid her scarred hand over Lindsey's cheek.

"It hasn't been that for years, Mom. You live there." Lindsey spoke as slowly and gently as she would to a child. Because she didn't possess any of her own, she figured she must have borrowed some of Dylan's patience and strength. His long, lean body hovered so near, his heat warmed her.

"You're doing great," he murmured by her ear.

Her mother shook her head. "No, no, I don't anymore. That was just for a little while and so long ago."

Lindsey brushed the hair back from her mother's face again. The sting of tears and guilt blinded her for a moment. "You've lived there nine years now, Mom."

Her mother laughed. "Lindsey, always spinning your yarns, just like your father."

"No, Mom…"

"Shh," her mother said, pressing a finger over Lindsey's lips. "Listen."

The radio newscaster reported Chet Oliver's death.

Her mother laughed again. "The old bastard. He deserved to die."

"What, Mom?"

"Selling babies the way he did—the bastard!" Then her laughter turned into hysterical sobbing.

Lindsey pulled her mother into her arms, more to restrain than to comfort. "Calm down, Mom."

"He stole babies, Lindsey..." Her body went limp, sagging heavily against Lindsey, as she fainted dead away.

Chapter Three

Dylan waited in the wide corridor outside Retha Warner's room at the sanatorium. Beside him, Lindsey leaned against the wall. She dragged the toe of her hiking boot back and forth over the squares of sparkling clean linoleum.

"You don't have to stay," she repeated. "Dad's here. He can give me a ride home, you know. I'll be fine if you leave. You have a lot going on with this murder and all."

He stepped in front of her and lifted her chin, so she would finally look him in the eye. Then he pressed a finger across her lips before she could say any more. "I'm staying."

He didn't know if he got through to her because the door behind him opened. Her father exhaled a ragged breath and brushed a hand through his thinning gray hair. "Is she all right, Mr. Warner?"

The older man nodded and took Dylan's arm. "They've sedated her. Thank you, Deputy, for finding her, for being there." Then William Warner reached out a hand toward his daughter, but Lindsey shook her head.

"Lindsey?"

"No, Dad. I want some answers for once. I want the real reason she's like that!" Lindsey straightened from the wall, bristling with anger. "I want to know why she called Chet Oliver a baby thief! You know, but you've never told me!"

Dylan had never seen Lindsey so distraught. But she wasn't the girl he'd once known. She was a woman now. Then he realized he'd never known the girl, either. "Lindsey, your father—"

"No." Mr. Warner sighed and shoved his trembling hands into his pockets. "She's right. You know about the miscarriages, Lindsey."

She nodded. "After me, she couldn't carry another baby to full term. She really wanted another baby, a boy...."

Bitterness dripped from Lindsey's words. Apparently she thought she'd never been enough to make her mother happy. While Dylan hated being involved in other people's emotional scenes, he found he couldn't detach himself from this one. When he held out a hand for her, she grasped it tightly in both of hers.

William Warner shook his head. "No, honey. She wanted a boy to replace the one she gave up a few years before we met at college. This place—" He waved his arms around the wide corridor.

"—used to be a home for unwed mothers," Lindsey finished. "That's what she meant when she said she'd been here long ago. She'd—"

"Been sent here by her parents when she became pregnant during her senior year of high school in Chicago. They wanted her to have the baby and give him up for adoption. She was to go off to college that fall. So she came to this place, but she didn't want to give up her baby.''

Despite his misgivings, Dylan found himself drawn into the story, into a young girl's loss. ''But she did.''

Warner nodded. ''Yes. Lindsey, I met your mother at college. When she heard I was from this town, well…''

Lindsey didn't say anything, but her fingers clutched Dylan's hand so tightly, he'd have indentations of her short, no-nonsense nails in his skin.

''She told me everything,'' Will Warner explained.

''What was 'everything,' Mr. Warner?'' Dylan asked. ''I mean, how did Chet Oliver figure into this?''

''He was the lawyer who handled the adoptions.''

''A baby broker. Is that legal?'' Lindsey's dark eyes widened.

''It was if your mother signed away her parental rights of her own free will,'' Dylan clarified. ''It would be considered a private adoption. A lot of people prefer them.''

''And if it wasn't of her own free will?'' Lindsey's dark eyes swam with her mother's pain and loss. ''Then you have a motive for Chet Oliver's murder. That's why you're here, huh, Dylan?'' She dropped his hand and whirled away.

''Lindsey!'' But she didn't stop. She stomped down the corridor, and the guard at the outside door didn't attempt to stop her.

"Is that true, Dylan?" Mr. Warner grabbed Dylan's arm again. "Is my wife a suspect?"

Dylan shrugged. "I don't know, sir. She left here early yesterday afternoon. She wasn't found until late this morning. Chet was murdered last night. No one can account for her whereabouts. I don't know."

LINDSEY DIDN'T GLANCE UP when Dylan approached her. She continued to balance one hip on the front bumper of the patrol car. With the toe of her hiking boot she pushed a couple of leaves across the asphalt. "What's that saying about going home again?" she asked.

"You can't do it." His tone was flat, unemotional. People said that about him. His mother died when he was still a boy, and with her had died Dylan Matthews's capacity for emotion. But Lindsey never believed what people said when it came to Dylan Matthews.

She shook her head. "Naw. It feels like it always did. Marge gossiping about me down at the diner. Mom having her episodes. Dad keeping his secrets. Naw. If this was ever really my home, then I came back to it. Why would I do something so stupid?"

His shadow fell across the asphalt at her feet. She glanced up, but he'd put on his sunglasses again. What did it matter? She'd never had a chance of reading his mind. But she was a reporter to her soul. She had to ask her questions. "Why would you?"

He expelled a breath through his nostrils. "Why would I come back? I had to do something about the house."

She raised a brow. "You can do better than that."

"There was nothing for me in Detroit."

"After ten years? No little woman to keep the home fires burning?"

He snorted now. "Yeah, right. What about you, Lindsey? Nobody for you?"

"The rumor is I came home with a broken heart, remember?" She forced the levity.

"Really?"

She almost believed he wanted to know. She shrugged. "You know the gossip in this town, only about half of it's ever true. I may be bruised, but I'm not broken."

Half his mouth lifted into a sexy smile. "Lindsey. Why are you home?"

"Nothing for me in Chicago. And maybe home is where the heart is, or the heartache." She sighed and dropped her gaze to the long shadow Dylan Matthews cast. He'd been there, a shadow across her heart, for the last ten years.

"I figured you had probably hot-wired my car and taken off. You were steamed in there, just a few minutes ago," he reminded her.

If she was smart, she would have. But she'd never been smart where Dylan was concerned. He would more than bruise her; he'd break her.

She nodded. "Yeah, I should have. But then you'd have to arrest me, and with my record..."

"You have a record now?"

She laughed over his shock. "Well, parking tickets. Didn't you expect that, after all those tickets you gave me?"

"I let you get away with warnings quite a few times."

"Yeah, I should have listened." To straighten away from the bumper, she held out a hand to him. He closed his long fingers over hers and pulled her up. He was too close, too tempting.

"Now I'm going to make you listen," she vowed.

"Hmm?" He pulled her closer.

Lindsey's foolish heart raced away from her. "Yeah, you're going to listen to me. My mother is not a suspect. That's ridiculous."

He dropped her hand and stepped around to the passenger's door, which he held open for her. "Murder is pretty ridiculous when you think about it, not an act of a rational person."

She agreed. She'd seen too many senseless deaths. "But not my mother's act. Someone else did this, and I'm going to prove it to you." She stepped close again, her face to his throat.

"Great." His breath stirred her bangs.

"Great?"

He gently pushed her into the seat. "Murder isn't my field. I was in the narcotics division."

"Narcotics?" She'd known some narcotics officers, tough, cynical people who lived life on the edge. She'd attended a couple of their funerals. She shuddered.

He closed the door and walked around to the driver's side. "There's just a couple things about this, Lindsey."

"Yeah?"

"You stay safe, all right? I don't want you running around stirring up a murderer."

She glared. "I'm careful."

He chuckled. "Yeah, right. You are going to be careful this time. I don't want you hurt."

Her heart softened. "And the other thing?"

"It stays out of the paper."

"What? I'm a reporter. That's—"

"You'll have the story after we have the murderer. You will not speculate in the paper."

She smiled. "If I did that, I'd have to print an article with my mother as a suspect. No, any speculating I do will go no further than your ears. Can I trust you, Dylan?"

HE NEVER ANSWERED HER. Lindsey found that oddly reassuring. If he'd adamantly maintained his trustworthiness, she would have doubted him. If he'd warned her against trusting him, she would have argued. As it was, he'd dropped her back at her Jeep, and they'd parted ways three days ago.

She'd been busy. And by staying busy, she'd kept her mind from straying into some painful areas. Stinging pride could not compare to the pain of her parents' betrayal. She had a brother, or so her mother claimed. And she'd never known.

She jerked the Jeep to a stop in Dylan's driveway and with it her runaway thoughts. It was early for some people, late for night owls. The sun was just a hint in a still-dark sky. Of course, it was autumn in northern Michigan. The sun took its time rising in autumn and rarely showed at all for winter.

Dylan was an early riser. She had missed him yesterday. She hadn't gone to the police station because she didn't want anyone overhearing and spreading rumors about her mother. The town gossiped about her mother too much as it was.

Lindsey threw open her door and inhaled a huge gulp of crisp morning air. Last night someone had burned leaves. Lindsey could taste the acrid smoke that drifted like fog just above the ground. Before her mother had tried to burn down the house, Lindsey had loved the aromatic smell of burning leaves. Now it left her with stinging eyes.

Kind of like the thought of having a brother. She, who had been so alone in her youth, had a brother. No, it wasn't possible. She shook off the crazy notion.

She grabbed her backpack from the passenger's seat and slung it over her shoulder. Her rubber soles were silent on the gravel drive as she strode to his door. But a metallic hammering sound reached her ears. She paused, her hand mid-reach, at the screen door.

Closing her eyes brought forth an image of Jimmy Matthews that night. Jimmy's murder had stolen Dylan's last relative. He was all alone now.

She inhaled a quick breath. Dylan wouldn't want her pity, just as she hadn't wanted his the day they had found her mother. He hadn't known how far from reality her mother had drifted. But murder? Could he really believe her mother capable of murder? She had to prove Retha Warner wasn't.

She pulled open the screen and knocked in rapid succession on the glass of the back door. The knob rattled with each strike of her fist. She grasped it in her hand and was surprised it turned beneath her palm.

He'd lived in Detroit for ten years. How did he dare to leave his door unlocked? She always made certain to dead-bolt hers.

"Dylan?" Cautiously she stepped inside. She automatically glanced to the floor, to the stain in front of the refrigerator. She shuddered. How could he live here?

"Dylan?" she called out again.

An assault of steel guitars and blows and guttural cries emanated from the basement. The maple floorboards vibrated beneath her feet from the racket. Was someone getting beat up to the accompaniment of music?

She found the door to the basement standing open and tiptoed down the stairs. The portable stereo on the bottom step vibrated with the volume of the heavy metal music pouring from it.

In the middle of the basement a huge bag hung from the rafters, and Dylan attacked the bag with his fists and feet.

He wore only the bottoms of his sweat suit and those were cut off at the knee. His muscular chest was bare and glistened with the perspiration of his labor as he hammered at the bag with his fists in boxing gloves. Muscles rippled in his arms and legs as he swung and kicked, the bag bouncing away from the strike of his worn-out running shoe.

She'd never seen him so focused but yet so out of control at the same time. As his fists and feet slammed into the bag with a frenzied speed, cries of rage broke through his lips. When she caught sight of his eyes, the glazed look of them frightened her.

Then his gaze tangled with hers, and the glaze vanished to be replaced by his usual impenetrable stare. "I'm following up my run with a workout on the bag," he said between gasping breaths.

She nodded and popped off the radio with the toe of her sneaker. "Is that what you're calling it? If I was that bag, I'd press charges against you."

"Maybe I should press some of my own. Breaking and entering, Ms. Warner?" He lifted a brow. Then he snagged his sweatshirt from the rusted lid of an old freezer and pulled it over his head.

She bit her lip to stop her protest of his covering his magnificent chest. A soft sigh escaped her lips. Before the shirt dropped to his waist, she noticed a jagged scar across one of his washboard abs.

"You left the door unlocked. Must have been some run. Good thing you do it before sunrise—you'd scare anyone meeting you on the street." She softened her words with a smile and held back the question about his scar.

He shook his head. "You don't seem very afraid of me, and you're exaggerating."

She laughed. "No, I'm not, but thank goodness the gossips are wrong about you." And thank goodness she'd been right. She'd always argued Dylan Matthews didn't lack feelings; he just kept them hidden from the prying eyes of this town. She was glad to finally be right about a man. But that didn't make him any less dangerous to her stupid heart. Actually, it made him more so.

"Should I care about the gossip?" His ironic tone suggested he didn't.

"I thought you did. I thought that's why you left this town a decade ago."

"Looking for a story, Ms. Reporter?" He grabbed a towel from the freezer and mopped his glistening face and scrubbed it over his sweat-darkened hair.

"Naw, you're old news," she scoffed, but it was a lie. Dylan Matthews was still as hot a topic as ever for conversation and idle sexual fantasies. She sighed.

He glanced up at her from under his towel. "You have anything new?"

She grinned, and he laughed. But the intense moment wasn't forgotten. Her nerves still tingled with excitement. Dylan Matthews was one smoking cauldron of hot emotions. She wanted to stir him up again.

"So smug, Lindsey. You must have something good. Can I trust you to make coffee while I grab a shower? The coffee and maker are on the counter." He joined her on the stairs.

From her perch above him, Lindsey relished the height advantage, something she rarely had. She peered down at him. "I'm your guest. You should make the coffee. And I could use some breakfast, too? Can you make eggs?"

He didn't stay below her. He sidled up so they shared the same step and pressed her between the concrete wall of the basement and the muscular wall of his chest. The jersey material had darkened with his sweat and the musk of man and perspiration filled her senses. The cold of the concrete seeped through the back of her sweater while his heat scorched her front.

"Usually my breakfast guests have spent the night, Lindsey. If that had been the case, I'd make you the most incredible breakfast." His voice had dropped to a low and intimate level.

Lindsey lifted her gaze to his face, only inches from hers, and batted her lashes. "If I'd spent the night with you, Dylan, you wouldn't have the strength to make breakfast."

His chuckle sounded strained, and he quickly brushed past her to climb the stairs.

"Dylan?" she called out. "You're walking a little funny. Did you strain something when you kicked that bag?"

"You strained something, you tease. Still playing, huh?" he grumbled.

"Who says I'm playing?"

DYLAN TWISTED THE FAUCET to cold and stood under the icy spray. But it wasn't enough to extinguish the fire in his blood. Lindsey Warner did something to him, and what was worse than his reaction to her was that she knew it.

He had a murder to solve, and her mother was the prime suspect. He couldn't get involved with her; it wouldn't be ethical.

But Lindsey didn't play by any rules. He stepped out of the shower stall to find the bathroom door half open. She reached around the door to place a mug on the rim of the sink. In the mirror, rapidly clearing of fog, he spied her wicked grin and dancing eyes.

"Lindsey," he threatened.

"Need any help, Deputy?" Her naughty chuckle grew fainter as she moved down the hall.

He kicked the door closed and stepped back into the shower stall to twist the faucet on to cold again.

His teeth chattered when he joined her in the kitchen. He'd wrapped his hands around the warm mug, but his fingernails were still blue. "You are such a tease!"

She jumped away from the sink, and a tinkle of ice on stainless steel rang out. He drew close enough to watch an ice cube disappear down the drain. "Hot?" He lifted a brow and detected a slight damp flush on her beautiful face.

"I always put ice in my coffee. I'm too impatient to wait for it to cool," she explained in a far-too-innocent-sounding voice.

He laughed. "I don't think anything manages to cool off around you. You never said what I'd done to deserve your torture this early in the morning."

"Torture? Not hardly. I came to make your life easier. I'm helping you solve your murder, Dylan."

He shivered. "Not *my* murder, Lindsey."

"You know what I mean." But for once her tone was a bit more serious. He followed her glance to the stain on the kitchen floor.

"Chet was a good man as far as I've heard."

"He was a baby thief," she argued.

"That's your mother's story." And her motive.

"And her motive." Lindsey spoke his thought

aloud. "Yeah, I know that. But other people had motives. I've found more suspects."

"You found the developer, right? Robert Hutchins. And if he has an alibi, he could have always sent his right-hand man, the mysterious Mr. Quade."

She glared at him, and he chuckled again. "Think I was just waiting for you to wrap this up for me? I may not know much about murder, but I know how to work a case."

"Hung out in Marge's, huh?" She snorted.

He grinned. "I take it that was your source of information, as well as cinnamon rolls. Of course, you reporters protect your sources."

"Nobody needs to protect Marge. She looks out for herself."

"She's a nice lady," Dylan defended.

"She's not been ragging on you since you got back," Lindsey grumbled. Then she shrugged. "Doesn't matter. I have other suspects. You have to see that my mother isn't the only one. And besides, the developer—"

"I really don't consider him a suspect," Dylan cut in.

"You don't?"

He leaned around her, grabbed the coffeepot and splashed some more dark liquid into his mug. She smelled of cinnamon and burning leaves. He took a deep breath, then quickly drew back. The soft purr of a car engine distracted him. Probably Mr. Smithers. He was the closest neighbor. "What?"

"You don't consider the developer a suspect?"

He shook his head. "No. He would have bought off someone like Chet, not killed him."

"Maybe he tried and Chet refused the money."

"A man who sold babies would refuse money for a zoning vote?"

"We haven't proved he sold babies. My mother has never been the most reliable source of information, you know."

"She told your father about the adoption when they first met. She didn't have any episodes until after several miscarriages following your birth."

She straightened from the sink and paced around his kitchen. "You've been checking out my mother?"

"That's pretty much common knowledge, Lindsey," he said softly, and caught her on her next circuit around the kitchen table. Her shoulder tensed beneath his hand, and he could trace the bones. She was more fragile than she liked to appear.

"This damn town and its gossips." Her breath hitched, and her lids dropped over her dark, sad eyes. When she opened them again, the sadness was gone. She shrugged off his hand.

"Lindsey, how do you feel about having a brother? Do you think it's true?"

"I don't know. If it isn't, my mother has no motive for murder. If it is, I have a brother." She lifted her arms and dropped them back to her sides. "I don't know what to think, let alone what to feel."

He understood. Separating thinking and feeling kept him sane. Perhaps Lindsey had a degree of detachment, too. "Let's find out what the truth is. I talked to Chet's nephew, who took over Chet's practice after his retirement. A few months ago, the office was broken into and some old files stolen. Chet was quite upset about it when Art Oliver told him.''

Lindsey didn't look surprised. ''You knew that,'' he guessed.

She nodded. ''I went to school with Art Oliver. So there's no record of those adoptions?''

''The sanatorium is looking for the old records from when it was the home for unwed mothers.''

''I hate the way that sounds. That alone had to be quite a stigma for any girl who was sent there.'' Lindsey ran her finger around the rim of her coffee cup, and Dylan suspected she thought of her mother's embarrassment and pain.

''I sense another story.'' Absently he noted the grind of an engine starting.

She sighed. ''Yeah, one I should have been more interested in long ago. Maybe I would have known the truth then.''

Dylan dragged in a deep breath and caught a whiff of gasoline. Had she fueled her tank before stopping by? Was it on her hands or did the rusty tank leak? She loved that Jeep because her dad had given it to her. ''Are you talking to your dad yet?'' She'd been so angry over her father's silence.

''Yeah. I've never been able to stop talking to my dad, but he knows I'm not happy with him.'' She sloshed some more coffee into her cup. A few droplets ran over the back of her hand.

He grabbed her wrist and brought her hand to his mouth. ''Did you burn yourself?''

She shook her head. "Naw, coffee's getting cold. Your pot is ancient."

He licked the droplets from her skin. "You're right. It is cold. Your hands are always cold."

She pulled her hand from his. "You know what they say. Cold hands, warm heart." She rubbed at her eyes.

Dylan smelled it then, the acrid smell of burning leaves and wood. "Smoke?"

"Someone must have been burning leaves around here. There was smoke when I drove up." Lindsey coughed. "But it's getting worse."

Dylan strode to the kitchen door to peer out. Flames had eaten the scraggly grass close to the house, forming a three-foot-high wall at his back door. His heart slammed into his ribs.

He grabbed the phone, but there was no dial tone. "Go out the front door, Lindsey. I'm going to grab the cell phone from my bedroom."

"Phone line's dead?" She rifled through her leather backpack and flipped open a cell phone. "Use mine."

"Outside. Use the front door." He didn't wait for her compliance but wrapped his hand around her elbow and ushered her through the living room.

The snap and crackle of the fire increased with their steps. He let out a ragged breath at the sight of the smoke billowing under the front door.

"Damn!" Lindsey cursed. She climbed over the back of his threadbare couch to the window and jerked up the blinds. Smoke and fingers of flames climbed over the ivy covering the windows.

Dylan grabbed her hand. "There's no time. Come on!" He pulled her to his bedroom.

Lindsey sighed. "All these years of my begging, Dylan, and now you finally drag me to your bed! Talk about picking your moment!"

"This isn't it, Lindsey." He yanked the comforter from the bed and dragged it and her into the shower stall across the hall. He got in and turned on the faucet, then wrapped the wet comforter around them both.

With care he led Lindsey through the smoke-filled house. He glanced once toward the kitchen and the blood-stained floor before he turned to the front door.

Lindsey's fingers clutched his back, her face buried in his neck as he lifted her in his arms. He wouldn't let her down as he'd let down Jimmy, his mother and his father. Smoke burned his lungs as guilt burned his soul.

Then he burst through the wall of flames.

Chapter Four

Dylan had never asked for her trust, but he had it. Lindsey penetrated a wall of fire with only his arms and a wet comforter wrapped around her.

He dragged her to the ground and rolled them around on the gravel drive where the fire had not reached. Lindsey tightened her arms around his neck and buried her nose farther in his neck.

He smelled of smoke, as did everything else. But she didn't care. She took a deep breath of acrid air, burning her throat and lungs. A cough racked her.

"Are you all right? Lindsey?" Dylan's soot-darkened hands cradled her face.

She marveled at his gentleness when only an hour ago he'd pummeled a punching bag with those huge, callused hands.

She nodded. "I'm fine. Right? I'm not on fire or anything?"

"Not anymore."

"That's reassuring." Her heart beat furiously and she fought the trembling in her body. Tears stung her eyes, and she didn't know if smoke or memories of another fire had evoked them. She glanced beyond him at the house, which was now fully engulfed.

She squirmed around, pulled her backpack from underneath them and dragged out her phone. "Quick. Call it in. Your house—"

"—is a lost cause." But he took the phone. "And your Jeep…"

Lindsey's gaze shot to her sweet-sixteen present from her dad. Flames ate at the rusted and dented metal. Dylan pulled her to her feet, and she stumbled with him farther from the fire.

Faintly, she heard him on the phone, as if he were talking in another room and not next to her. He reported the fire and dropped the phone back in her bag.

He wrapped his arms around her from behind, linking his hands at her waist. Naturally she leaned into his muscled chest. "I'll miss that Jeep, too." His breath whispered into her ear, and his heart pounded heavily against her back.

Lindsey gave up the battle and let the tears fall. "Your house… How stupid, all this destruction because someone was burning some leaves."

"Hmm," was Dylan's vague reply.

"What?" asked her reporter's instinct.

"Smell that."

"Smoke."

"What kind?"

Lindsey took a deep breath and sputtered again. "Leaves. Wood. The rubber tires and…"

"Gasoline."

"From my Jeep?"

"No, by the house. I smelled it earlier, just before the smoke."

His voice was as calm as always, but she knew what she'd find in his eyes. She tipped up her head and looked into the glazed rage she'd seen in the basement while he had pummeled the bag.

"Dylan, you can't mean this was intentional, that it was deliberately set."

"Maybe. Off the record, between two people who were almost toast, maybe. On the record, someone might have used gasoline to start his damp leaves burning. It's possible."

"It's stupid."

"Yeah, too stupid and too close to my house."

But his house was gone. She heard the tinkling of glass as the windows shattered and the flames licked the house inside out. It was gone.

DYLAN PERCHED ON THE corner of his desk in the police station and kept an eye on Lindsey where she stood in the hall, talking on her cell phone. He hadn't taken his eyes off her since the fire. She could have been killed. He could have let her down as badly as he had everyone else. But they'd been lucky this time.

"So." He turned to Sheriff Buck, who hovered at his side. "You checked with the sanatorium?"

The sheriff matched his quiet tones, no easy feat for the big man with the naturally booming voice. "Retha Warner was in her room the entire time, heavily sedated. There's no way she was anywhere else."

Dylan nodded. "Good." He couldn't imagine

Lindsey's pain if she discovered her mother had set this fire, too.

"Old man Smithers was burning leaves late last night. He's not far from your place. He doesn't know if it was completely out when he went to bed. It was probably just an accident, Dylan. A terrible accident."

Dylan knew about those. He glanced at the sheriff, at the soft look in the older man's eyes. He'd been there for Dylan then, too. "Yeah, you're probably right."

"This is Winter Falls. People don't do those kinds of things here."

Lindsey joined them. "What? Commit murder? Ask Chet Oliver about that, Sheriff."

Dylan drank her in. Her black curls had wilted and lost some of their gloss. Her delicately featured face was smeared with soot, and her eyes had lost a bit of their sparkle but none of their sass.

"Hope you have insurance, Deputy," she said, but her fingers skimming lightly over the back of his hand softened the callousness of her words.

"What about you?"

She shrugged. "Couldn't afford the premiums for full coverage."

"You said parking tickets. You don't get points for those." He managed to lift his lips into a teasing smile.

"Maybe a few speeding, too." She winked, but the mascara and soot smeared around her eyes stole the sexiness from the gesture. Nevertheless, his pulse quickened.

"And you must have checked on my mother. You know she never left the sanatorium."

"It was an accident, Lindsey," the sheriff cut in. "Nobody was at fault."

She snorted. "Yeah. That's easy for you to say. You didn't nearly charbroil."

Dylan laughed. "I can't wait to read your article on this."

"Been reading my byline, Dylan?"

She'd been careful in her coverage of Chet's death. Everything had been inconclusive and under investigation.

She'd also done a story on the battle over the new mall. She'd not been able to get the developer's side of the story, though. Dylan couldn't imagine she hadn't tried.

"So you're working for your dad, then, Lindsey?" the sheriff asked.

Lindsey nodded. "Yup. I'm a reporter covering a story, Sheriff. There's a story here."

Before the sheriff could bellow out a protest, Dylan clamped a hand on Lindsey's wrist and turned to the older man. "Don't worry, Sheriff. It's under control."

The sheriff shook his balding head. "You're smarter than to think that, boy."

"You talking about me? You think you have me under control?" Lindsey smiled. He didn't like the wicked gleam in her dark brown eyes.

"I wouldn't be so foolish," Dylan protested. "Come on. Let me drop you home." He'd been lucky enough to shower and change into his uniform at the station. Lindsey was still dirty, but she didn't complain, as other women he'd known would have.

She glanced down at herself and grimaced. "I guess I'm a sight."

Before Dylan could grab his keys from his desk, William Warner burst through the doors of the station. Despite her grime, he caught his daughter tightly in his arms and buried his face in her hair.

"I'm so glad you're okay," he whispered.

"Have I got a story for the next edition," Lindsey quipped, but Dylan spied the hint of tears in her eyes.

For an eloquent newspaper editor, Will Warner only muttered a few incoherent words. "I'll drive us home, Dad," Lindsey said, and shot Dylan a look over her father's shoulder.

Dylan nodded. Lindsey's father needed her. After the auto accident that had killed Dylan's mother, his father had never needed him. A handful of years later, he'd managed to drink himself to death.

With an effort he pulled himself from the depths of self-pity where he was tempted to drown. He hated to see Lindsey leave.

But he wasn't really alone. The sheriff had always been there for him, had always cared about him. Even when his own father hadn't.

The sheriff slapped a hand on Dylan's shoulder after the Warners left the station. "That girl's always been trouble." Dylan didn't need the reminder.

LINDSEY SLUMPED in her corner booth at Marge's Diner and ducked behind her newspaper. She had been there long enough that people had forgotten her presence. Conversation flowed around her with the late afternoon sunshine.

Rumor had it that Dylan had burned down his own house. And more than one person was suspicious of his involvement in Chet Oliver's death. How was it the old lawyer was murdered on Dylan's first day back on the job? And just after Chet Oliver had been in Marge's Diner claiming he had something for Dylan from Steve Mars.

Lindsey wanted to know that, too. She wanted to know a lot of things about Dylan Matthews. Some of it had been revealed to her when she'd peeked in his bathroom mirror yesterday. She let out a ragged breath and fanned herself with a corner of the paper. The man was built.

Her paper snapped forward, and she noticed conversation had stopped. She lowered the paper and discovered Dylan's handsome face. He wore the dark glasses again. But instead of his uniform, he wore a denim shirt with the cuffs rolled to his elbows and faded jeans.

"Very Sam Spade." He smirked as he slid into the booth opposite her.

"I didn't cut eyeholes into it," she defended herself.

"But you were tempted."

She shrugged. "I haven't been gone so long that I've forgotten voices." She glanced around at their interested observers and offered a few glares.

She'd had to control her sharp tongue when they'd maligned Dylan's character. She knew he hadn't set the fire, but what else did she really know about him?

She stared at the twin reflections of herself in his dark glasses. Reflected back was a vulnerable woman who too easily believed the image, the veneer, but never knew the core of a man. She'd been burned before. She wouldn't be that foolish again.

Wasn't Dylan just a man? No hero, no white knight? He was capable of rage. She'd seen it. She had to remember he was not the perfect image she'd created in her youth. But yesterday he'd saved her from a fire.

"So you hear the rumor?" she asked in a loud voice.

"What's that?"

"You torched your own house. Wanted the insurance money. What? You going to make a million off that old place?" She flashed another glare at a particularly outraged listener.

Before Dylan could comment, Marge bustled over to their table with a pot of coffee. She turned over the cup in front of Dylan and filled it. Then she splashed a bit more in Lindsey's cooling cup. "You don't need any more caffeine, missy." She tsked.

Lindsey grimaced.

Marge smoothed a hand over her apron. "But people have been talking foolish, Dylan. The girl's right about that. Everybody should know you wouldn't burn down your old family place, not after having kept it all these years."

Lindsey slid her fingers over Marge's hand. The older woman had seen what Lindsey had not, and she was supposed to be a professional observer.

Dylan had hung on to his home despite all the bad

memories surrounding it. Because it was his home. Unlike her childhood home that had only been briefly scarred by fire and then rebuilt, his was only ashes now.

She waited until Marge bustled away with a promise to bring Dylan a slice of pie. Under the table she rubbed her knee against his.

"You okay? Where you staying?"

Dylan smiled but didn't remove the dark glasses. "The sheriff put me up. He has a pullout bed in his den. Of course, I feel like I'm in a taxidermy shop. There are stuffed critters and fish mounted all over the walls. I go to sleep with all those eyes watching me."

Lindsey had to laugh. "I wouldn't be able to sleep at all. I'd be afraid of them laughing at my snoring or something."

Dylan rubbed his knee farther up her thigh. "You snore?" Disappointment deepened his voice. "Well, that's it. You and I can never be."

Was he joking, or did he mean it? And why should she care either way? "You must have said that to me a million times all those years ago."

Dylan chuckled. "I should have sued you for sexual harassment."

Marge joined in his laughter as she slid a plate of Dutch apple pie next to his coffee cup. "She still giving you trouble, Dylan?"

"She's just jealous, Marge. She knows you've already stolen my heart." He patted the older woman's hand. The fifty-something blond woman faintly blushed and laughed.

Lindsey rolled her eyes.

Marge turned to her. "Hear anything new about the developers? They were in yesterday—the rich guy and his young right-hand man. Never had such big operators in this place before. Cell phones. Laptop computers…"

"Yesterday?" The day of the fire. The pungent odor of it still clung to Lindsey's curls. She'd washed and rinsed over and over, but still the scent lingered and haunted her.

She'd not slept the night before as images of a different outcome had chased through her mind. And this fire had blended into the other, and she, Dylan and her mother had all been lost to the flames.

Dylan leaned across the booth and touched her face. "You okay?"

She nodded in sharp jerks. "Yeah, yeah. I'm fine. Some coincidence, though. When were they here, Marge?"

"Morning. Pretty early. They had a meeting with the trustees. Now there's only Mayor Reynolds opposing the new development. Chet's nitwit nephew inherited his seat on the board. He's already been bought off."

"Marge," Dylan cautioned.

"I'm not making unfounded accusations, Dylan," she defended. "It's a fact. Art Oliver is handling some of their legal business now."

Lindsey jotted a note on a legal pad at her elbow. "I'll ask him about that."

"Who?" Dylan picked up his fork.

"Evan Quade, the right-hand man. I'm interviewing him in about thirty minutes." She'd have to drive her mom's car. Borrowing it unsettled her, but Retha Warner had no further use of the old Bonneville.

"What?" Dylan pushed away his plate. "I don't want you going alone to see this man. Where are you meeting him?"

Lindsey narrowed her eyes and leaned back in the booth. "At his office in Traverse City."

"By the time you get there it'll be after hours. No way. You're not going." His fingers caught her wrist.

"Thinking about handcuffing me?" She turned her wrist in his grasp. "You're going to have to if you think you're stopping me from doing my job."

His deep blue eyes narrowed. "We talked about this, Lindsey. I don't want you stirring anyone up with your questions. This is a murder investigation."

"Oh, really? And I thought I was reporting on the local bake sale." She stuffed her notepad in her leather bag and slung the strap over her shoulder. When she stood, so did Dylan, his tall, lean body blocking her exit.

Marge stepped between them and reached for the pie. "Let me box this for you."

Dylan waved her away with a folded bill. "Thanks, Marge, but I'm not letting her go off alone. And I'm definitely not letting her drive, so I won't have time to eat it."

Lindsey gritted her teeth. She really hated being told what she could or could not do. "It's not up to you to let me do anything, Dylan. I do what I want. Have been for a long while. What do you think I did in Chicago? You don't think I ever got myself into a tight situation there?''

He brushed a hand through his hair, tousling the golden strands. ''Knowing you, I'm sure you did get in trouble.''

''And I got myself out.'' She caught him with her bag as she pushed past him and slipped through the door. A jerk on her shoulder strap pulled her up short.

He ran his fingers up the leather strap to her shoulder. Then his fingers slid over her cheek, his touch as warm and soft as the late afternoon sunshine washing over her face.

''Lindsey, I don't want you to get hurt.''

She opened her mouth to protest, but he slid his fingers over her lips, pressing them closed.

''I know you can take care of yourself. But this is my investigation. I don't want you putting yourself in danger over it. I'm going with you.''

Her lips curved beneath his fingers. She wanted to taste him, but she restrained herself. ''He didn't agree to a police interview.''

''I'm off duty.''

''So you're what? My assistant?''

He laughed. ''I'll be your driver. That's something I don't trust you doing.'' With his hand cupping her shoulder, he guided her to his black Expedition, parked by the curb.

His garage had been spared from yesterday's blaze. Miraculously his vehicle had survived with all its spit and shine. She wished her Jeep had been so lucky.

''Miss your Jeep?'' He held the passenger door for her.

She sighed. "Yeah. It was costing me a fortune in repairs and insurance, but I miss it."

"Yeah, me, too." He closed the door behind her and walked around to the driver's side.

When he slid into the seat beside her, Lindsey leaned over to brush a kiss across his cheek.

"What was that for?" He touched his skin where her lips had been.

She slid her fingers down his strong chin. "For thinking of me when you lost so much more."

He shrugged and turned the key in the ignition. "I should have sold it years ago. It was just a house. They've all been gone so long."

"You were what? Twelve? When your mother died…" The horror of the car accident that had cost him his mother was Winter Falls legend.

She doubted he'd answer her. She couldn't read his eyes behind the dark lenses, but he faced the road and seemed intent on the small-town traffic.

"Yes. We'd gone out for her birthday. Dad had too much to drink. She tried to get the keys from him, but he insisted he was fine. He wasn't."

Despite her reporter's soul, it wasn't why she had to know more. She had to know the man and the heart of the man. Perhaps heroes did exist. "And you were trapped in the back seat?"

"The sheriff got me out. Jimmy wasn't there. He'd skipped school that day, so Mom made him stay home." Did he envy Jimmy? After years on the police beat, she could imagine what he had seen from the back seat. Her heart ached for him.

"The sheriff was there when your dad died, too?"

"The sheriff's always been there." Affection softened his deep voice. "People say he wanted to marry my mom, but she chose my dad instead. He never married. I think he always loved her."

Lindsey smiled at the romanticism in a man outsiders considered incapable of emotion. "The sheriff's a good guy," she agreed.

"He's really upset about Chet. I have to find out who did this. And I really have only one solid lead." He turned briefly to her, then back to the road.

"My mother." She sighed and tamped down the little catch of fear in her heart. He had to be wrong.

HUTCHINS ENTERPRISES occupied an entire warehouse that had been converted to opulent offices. From the top floor, the clear blue Grand Traverse Bay stretched out below, sparkling in the glow of the late afternoon sun.

Dylan took an appreciative deep breath as he and Lindsey were escorted into the office of Robert Hutchins's right-hand man, Mr. Evan Quade.

The dark-haired man stood before the windows, gazing out over the bay below him.

"In an hour the sun will set over the water. It's a spectacular sight."

He turned toward his guests. "Ms. Warner, I've been looking forward to our interview. We've been having the *Winter Falls Gazette* delivered to our office, and you have a most remarkable turn of phrase."

She laughed, and the rich ripple of it tightened the muscles in Dylan's stomach. "Is that a nice way of calling me a hack?"

"Hardly. I wouldn't have agreed to this interview if I thought you couldn't be fair." His dark gaze swung toward Dylan. His eyes narrowed.

Dylan smiled. "Deputy Dylan Matthews."

Lindsey sighed.

"Deputy Matthews. We haven't met, but I've heard about you." His deep voice hinted at what rumors he'd heard. "I'm sorry we haven't been able to match our schedules, so I could answer your questions."

"It would probably help if you returned my calls."

Over the days since Chet Oliver's murder, Dylan had done some checking. He'd heard rumors, too. When he "officially" interviewed Quade, he'd figure out the truth about those rumors. Until then he would not trust the man alone with Lindsey.

When Quade turned back to Lindsey, he lifted a dark brow. "I think there's been a misunderstanding, Ms. Warner. I thought you were coming here on behalf of the paper to discuss Hutchins Enterprises mall proposal."

"I am." She dragged out her notepad.

"And why are you here, Deputy?"

Dylan let his gaze slide over Lindsey, from her unruly black curls to her scuffed hiking boots. "To keep an eye on an old friend."

He had to ensure her safety. But he didn't doubt she could take care of herself. He'd checked out her history in Chicago. Officers on the local force spoke highly of her, and he didn't know many police officers who thought highly of reporters. Absently he ran his hand over his stomach and fingered the jagged scar beneath the coarse material of his denim shirt.

"Personal, then?" Quade lifted a dark brow again and straightened the crease in his suit sleeve.

Dylan nodded. "For now." A time would come when he had to ask those official questions. But not now, not with Lindsey present.

"I'm really not here so much to discuss your development as the opposition to it," Lindsey began.

By scheduling an appointment late in the day, Quade had not given Lindsey much time. He'd not offered them seats. He leaned against the front of his massive desk, and they stood before him.

Even while Dylan resented it, he could admire the other man's control. He had no intention of answering her questions. Of course, the man had never met Lindsey before.

"I'd rather talk about the mall itself. It will be an enormous boon to this area, to the economy by way of increased tourism and employment opportunities." Dylan glanced at the man's hands. Did he have notes scribbled on them? From his rehearsed little speech, Dylan wouldn't have doubted it.

She wrote something on her pad. "I'm sure you have information on the mall project, the number of shops and names of them. But that's not what Winter Falls cares about right now. Chet Oliver's murder is what's news. He was one of the trustees opposed to the new mall. Now he's dead."

Dylan groaned and wrapped his fingers around Lindsey's arm. He'd warned her about stirring up a suspect. She'd just put the man in a blender.

Quade straightened his stance and the fit of his tailored suit. He dropped the facade of charming businessman. "We have a team of lawyers, Ms. Warner. I wouldn't want to have them file a libel suit against you, but there's no telling what Mr. Hutchins could decide if you go any further with this."

"I will not print any part of this investigation until there's a suspect in custody." Lindsey jerked her elbow from Dylan's hold.

Dylan hadn't accepted it as fact. He'd been burned before when he'd trusted a reporter. "Lindsey, Mr. Quade has no obligation to answer your questions. When he's officially questioned, he will be entitled to legal representation, and there will be no reporter present."

Quade chuckled and eased back against his desk. "Thank you, Deputy, for reading me my rights."

"That's not it at all—"

"Dylan! You promised you wouldn't interfere...."

Dylan shook his head. "I never promised that."

"Hey, kids." Quade held up a hand. "I'm curious. Ms. Warner, what would you like to know?" But he glanced at his wristwatch again.

Dylan smiled over the not-so-subtle hint.

Lindsey pressed her pen to her pad. "When was the last time you had contact with Chet Oliver?"

"On behalf of Mr. Hutchins, I met with Mr. Oliver at his home a few days before his death. We were to attend the monthly Winter Falls township meeting, which was being held yesterday. Initially we wanted to see if we could reach a compromise with Mr. Oliver."

"Compromise?" Lindsey asked.

Quade nodded. "Perhaps there was an alternative

location he would prefer to the proposed site. There's a lot of vacant farmland around Winter Falls. We have an option to purchase the three hundred acres on the main road, but if Oliver's concerns regarded increased road congestion, there were other suitable sites we could option.''

Quade plucked at the crease in his trousers. ''Our meeting was amicable. He was impressed that we were open to his suggestions. He promised to consider approving some alternative sites we suggested. We parted on friendly terms.''

Lindsey snorted. ''Any witnesses to this amicable exchange?''

Quade narrowed his dark eyes. ''No. It was only Mr. Oliver and myself. I left the township surveys on his desk with the alternative locations marked. We even made some notes on them. He promised to consider them.''

''Nothing like that was found.'' Dylan's search of the lawyer's home and old office had been extensive.

''And why would whoever killed him take those notes?'' Lindsey added.

Quade risked a wrinkle in his tailored suit with a shrug. ''I couldn't answer that, Ms. Warner. I am unfamiliar with the workings of the criminal mind.''

Dylan nodded and bit off the remark about the businessmen he'd known being crooks. Lindsey had already antagonized the man.

''Thank you for your time, Mr. Quade.'' Dylan extended his hand. The strength of the businessman's grip and the roughness of his palm surprised Dylan.

"I have more questions," Lindsey objected. "Where were you the night of Chet Oliver's death?"

"Lindsey." Dylan's warning was wasted. He should have brought a muzzle.

Evan Quade chuckled. "Who's asking? The cop or the reporter?"

Dylan pushed his hand through his hair and almost wished he'd let Lindsey come alone. But Evan Quade wasn't a man he'd trust easily, with business or a beautiful woman. Especially this beautiful woman. "This is not a police interview, Mr. Quade."

"It's my interview." Lindsey lifted her chin.

Quade risked another wrinkle with a shrug. "Actually, Mr. Hutchins and I were working late that night. You can ask the security guard on your way out. He clocks in everyone's arrival and departure times."

Dylan nodded. "Let me try this again, Mr. Quade. Thank you for your time." He escorted Lindsey to the door. Over his shoulder he said, "See that you return my calls. I do need to speak with you in an official capacity."

"Interested in investing in the mall?" A smirk slid over the businessman's face.

Dylan chuckled. "Not on my salary."

Lindsey managed to wriggle around and shoot one last question at Quade. "Where does Mr. Hutchins live? I'd like to interview him, too."

Quade flashed a fierce glare. "Mr. Hutchins does not receive visitors at his home. If you would like to speak with him, he will be in the office at approximately eight-thirty tomorrow morning. To be honest, though, Ms. Warner, he never talks to reporters.''

Dylan nodded and pulled Lindsey into the reception area. He closed Quade's office door and caught Lindsey in his arms.

She sputtered out a couple of protests, which he silenced with his mouth. His lips took hers, moving over the smooth, satin flesh.

Instead of pushing him away, she placed her hands around his neck and pulled him closer. A murmur emanated from her throat. Even in a kiss, the woman was unable to stop talking. But he took advantage of her parted lips to slip his tongue inside and taste the sweetness of her.

Shaken by the depth of his desire for her and remembering where they were, he lifted his mouth from hers.

''What was that for?'' Her dark eyes narrowed.

He wanted to laugh, but his heart pounded too hard for amusement. ''To stop some of those.''

''What?'' She brushed a hand through the curls his fingers had tangled.

''Questions.''

She flashed him a glare. ''You stopped me before I was through with all mine. You completely destroyed my interview. I got nothing.''

He ran a hand through his mussed hair. ''Lindsey, that was supposed to be an interview? It was more like an interrogation. You're a reporter, not a cop.''

''I'm an investigative reporter after a story. Evan Quade knows more than he's saying.'' She turned for the elevator. Dylan spied her touching her thoroughly kissed lips.

He smiled and swallowed his admission that she was probably right. Where was the sense in encouraging her? If she pursued this story with as much passion as she had pursued him ten years ago, she'd risk more than bruised pride. She'd risk her life.

Chapter Five

Lindsey tucked a cocktail napkin in her jeans pocket. With a cocky smile on her face she sauntered to her table and slid into the booth across from Dylan.

He didn't raise his eyes from the beer cradled in his hands. "Done yet?" His harsh tone brought an edge to the question.

"What do you mean?"

"You don't know?" He raised his deep blue eyes, and she glimpsed a fraction of the rage they'd held when he'd pummeled the bag in the basement.

"What?"

"You're an unconscionable flirt!" The blue eyes flashed.

Lindsey allowed her cocky smile to slip into a grimace of outrage, but her heart was light. He was jealous! Dylan Matthews was jealous over her! If only he had shown that much interest when she was sixteen.

"Don't act outraged." He snorted. "You know it. You enjoy it. You just charmed the bartender out of his phone number. You don't think he's given it to every single and not-so-single woman who entered this bar tonight?''

Lindsey widened her eyes in feigned innocence. ''You think?''

Dylan snorted again. ''Jimmy was a bartender, remember? He slept with every woman who entered Good Times Tavern.''

Lindsey nodded. ''And some who didn't.''

''What do you mean?''

She shrugged. ''It doesn't matter. Jimmy's dead. Why talk about his conquests?''

''Not you?'' Now the outrage was his and obviously not feigned.

''Heck, no.'' Back then she'd only wanted Dylan. ''It's nothing. Rumors. You know how accurate those are.''

''Rumors are what killed him. People told Steve Mars that Jimmy was sleeping with his fiancée. Jimmy wouldn't have done that,'' Dylan maintained. Desperation and denial darkened his blue eyes.

''That rumor might have been wrong. There were others.''

Dylan shook his head. ''Rumors...''

Lindsey nodded and wisely withheld her argument. ''Doesn't matter now. That was a long time ago.'' But she suspected it wasn't to Dylan. ''I wonder what happened to his family.''

''They moved away, too?'' Dylan's eyes brimmed with pain.

''Yeah, shortly after you did. His fiancée left town before you. Then Steve's parents and his sister. They were adopted, you know, from Arborview when it was still the home for unwed mothers. Sarah is his sister's name. She was in my class.'' With a trembling hand she picked up her wineglass and swirled around the dark red liquid.

Dylan narrowed his eyes. "What?"

"I'm rambling." She sighed. When Chet Oliver's murder was solved, she had another story to investigate. And she hadn't even planned on staying in town.

"You were thinking about your mother, about what she said." His gaze was intent on her face. "That you could have a brother."

She shivered. "I don't know what to think. I'm going to investigate it as I would any other story."

Dylan nodded. "You'll find out the truth. You're a good reporter, Ms. Warner."

"If I was a good reporter, I'd have asked you about something long before now."

He raised a brow and picked up his mug of beer. Only a few bubbles rose to the surface, having already gone flat while she'd talked to the bartender.

"About?"

She twirled her wineglass again and stared into the red liquid, vividly remembering the puckered flesh across the tight muscles of his well-developed abdomen. Instead of asking the question she'd intended, she blurted out, "How did you get that scar?"

Dylan sighed. "I trusted someone I shouldn't have."

Lindsey's stomach tightened. She reached for his hand that lay on the table, covering it with hers. "A woman?" She'd trusted someone she shouldn't have. She'd believed his lies, worn his ring.

Dylan ran his fingers over the condensation on his beer mug. His chuckle echoed bitterly. "Not a woman. A reporter, one who asked too many questions."

She flinched. "A reporter? And you were hurt?"

"I thought he was a friend. My cover was blown by his narcotics exposé." He sighed. "It was time to get out, anyway."

"Time to come home?"

He laughed. "I'm not so sure about that. I probably should have come back sooner. Doesn't matter how much time passes, this town never forgets."

She nodded. "Is it okay if I ask more questions?"

His mouth twisted into a wry smile. "You're not going to blow my cover, Lindsey. But I still don't consider you safe."

"Safe?" She laughed. "I should hope not." She twirled her wineglass. "But that wasn't what I wanted to ask you."

He nodded. "Your dad mentioned what Chet Oliver was saying in the diner the day he died?"

"My dad?" Lindsey wrinkled her forehead. "What about my dad?"

"He was there, in the diner, when Chet came in and talked to the sheriff."

"Chet said he had something for you from Steve Mars." Her dad had never mentioned it. "Dad must have forgotten."

"He's a reporter. I didn't think your type forgot anything."

No, Lindsey never did, and she suspected her father didn't, either. Just one more secret he'd kept from her.

"It doesn't matter where I heard it. So what was it, and why didn't you tell me about it before now?"

Dylan shrugged. "I wish I knew what it was. If he had anything, I couldn't find it."

"You really don't want my help." Lindsey struggled to control her frustration but knew it had seeped into her voice.

Dylan's gaze dropped to the beer in his hand. "I never said that."

"But you don't trust me." She should have insisted on interviewing Quade alone.

He ran a finger around the rim of the mug. "How could something from a man who died ten years ago have anything to do with Chet Oliver's murder? Chet had whatever it was for ten years—"

"But maybe nobody knew until that day in the diner," Lindsey cut in.

Dylan shook his head. "Could a man keep a secret in this town?"

She nodded. "Apparently this man had no problem keeping secrets—letting sleeping dogs lie, as it were."

Dylan blew out an agitated breath. "I wish he'd given me some clue what it was, so I'd know if it was a motive for murder. Without it…"

Her heart plummeted. "My mother has the most compelling motive."

"Nobody's blaming your mother, Lindsey. We're looking at all the suspects." He slid his fingertips over her knuckles. "In a letter I received before I left Detroit, Chet said he had something for me. He knew

I was coming back and intended to give it to me then. But he never got the chance.''

Dylan's frustration was etched in the furrows in his brow. He had questions about his brother's death. He wanted to know what Jimmy had done to drive his best friend to murder. Perhaps the only man who could have given him some answers had been murdered. Why?

Uncomfortable with their discussion, she wriggled the cocktail napkin from her pocket and slid it over to him.

"His address, and you're giving it to me?'' Dylan toyed with the edge of the paper.

"Hutchins's address.''

"He doesn't receive visitors at home.'' His voice dripped sarcasm.

"Yeah, that bothered me, too. Since we're still in Traverse City, we might as well poke around some more. It would be a waste to come all this way and not interview Hutchins, too.'' Lindsey quirked her eyebrows at Dylan.

He shook his head. "You're relentless. He's not going to let you in, Lindsey. He doesn't talk to reporters.'' He pushed the napkin toward her.

Lindsey slid her hands off the table. "He'll talk to you.'' And hopefully, Dylan would let her tag along.

Dylan ran a hand over his denim shirt. "No uniform. He won't.''

"That lawsuit threat didn't spook you?'' She'd always considered Dylan invincible, fearless. She had to remember that image wasn't real, just a girlish fantasy.

A smile tipped up a corner of his mouth. "You're not going along on my police interviews."

She narrowed her eyes. "Have you done any? You didn't ask Quade any questions."

"Not in front of a reporter."

"Talk to Hutchins. You might get more with an 'unofficial' interview." And she might get some of what Dylan learned out of him.

He laughed. "You don't give up."

"I'm a reporter."

His hand slid over his stomach. "I'm not likely to forget."

She'd never get his trust. Her heart slowed despite the scent of victory. And without his trust, there would be no future for them. With a trembling hand she reached for her wineglass. What was she thinking? She'd given up on futures. Day by Day was her motto now.

"Okay."

The victory. "You'll talk to him now."

He reached for the napkin. "On our way home. If he doesn't want to talk without a lawyer, it'll wait."

She summoned some enthusiasm, reaching for her leather bag. His fingers closed over hers. "Your pad stays in the truck. With you."

WHAT HAD HE LET HER talk him into? Before he stepped through the door that had begrudgingly opened with the show of his badge, he glanced back at his SUV, which he'd parked behind a white Lincoln. Fog swirled around it, but he glimpsed Lindsey's shiny curls, her head bent over her notepad.

When he was through, she was going to grill him. He turned to follow the uniformed maid down the marble hallway. She opened French doors and stepped back.

Dylan walked into an enormous library. Leather-bound books lined the walls interspersed with some sculptures of varying sizes and materials. Power scented the air, its odor overwhelming.

Dylan had smelled it before in the homes of king-pin drug dealers. His nostrils flared, and the short hairs on the back of his neck rose.

"Deputy Matthews."

Dylan turned toward the windows and the desk before it. No light shined on the polished surface. The only lamp burned from a library table on the other side of the room.

In the gathering darkness, Dylan peered at the man of indeterminate age. Silver strands threaded through his dark hair. Did any lines mar his face? "Mr. Hutchins."

"I believe Mr. Quade informed you that I don't accept visitors in my home. And that was some time ago, at a decent hour." The man glared.

"I'm sorry, Mr. Hutchins. Chet Oliver's death has deeply shaken the residents of Winter Falls. If you can help us at all, it would be greatly appreciated." Dylan forced himself not to gag over the placating words when he really wanted to demand answers.

That was the downside to small-town police work, the politics. Yet, he hadn't found the situation any better in the anonymity of the big city.

Hutchins cleared his throat. "I doubt I'll be able to

help you. Quade told you the situation. He met with Oliver at my request. They were working on alternative sites for the mall development. We were willing to compromise, as was Mr. Oliver. This small project is irrelevant to Hutchins Enterprises.''

"There's money involved. If you don't build the mall, you'll lose some.'' He glanced around the library again, at the Oriental rug covering the polished floor, at the Impressionist painting hiding what was probably a wall safe.

Hutchins shrugged. "The option on the land isn't sizable. The owner only receives a large payment if the property is rezoned. Quade is a real estate lawyer. He advises me on such matters, so we don't lose much money if the town opposes a development.''

Dylan nodded and picked up a figurine from the sofa table. The porcelain was cold but smooth. Like Lindsey's skin.

"I've checked you and Quade out.''

Hutchins waited in silence.

He set the figure down. "I've heard some interesting things.''

"I could say the same of you, Deputy.''

Dylan winced and wished the town believed in him. By solving this murder, he hoped to prove that he was an honorable lawman.

"Opposition to your past developments has always changed their minds. Your original proposals pass. So who's compromising, Mr. Hutchins, if you always get what you want?''

The older man laughed. "I'm very persuasive, Deputy. Is that a crime?''

Dylan rubbed his chin. "Being persuasive? No, but murder is."

"Are you implying I killed Mr. Oliver?" Anger vibrated in his deep voice.

"No."

"Has anyone who's opposed me in the past been murdered?"

Dylan shrugged. "A couple vanished."

The older man laughed again. "With big checks and a determination to keep it out of the clutches of the IRS. That's their crime, not mine."

"So you just throw money at people to get your way?"

"Money talks." Hutchins picked up a paperweight from his desk, a Fabergé egg. Wrinkles and age marks lined his hands.

"So you could pay people to influence other people?" Dylan stepped closer to the desk, trying to get a good look at the man's face.

"Hire muscle, if you will?" His laugh rang out. "That's ridiculous."

"I've seen it done, Mr. Hutchins." And had the scars to prove it, some emotional as well as the physical.

His head bobbed. "That's right. You've been away from Winter Falls for a while. Quade told me."

"Quade. He's a strange man for you to hire."

"A real estate lawyer? He's the ideal man for me to hire."

"He was unemployable for a while. No one would take a chance on him. He must be grateful to you for giving him a job.'' And something about Quade's dark eyes bothered Dylan. They held secrets.

The thin shoulders in the cashmere sweater shrugged. ''I trust him. Is there anyone you trust, Deputy?''

The sheriff. No one else. Not even Lindsey. Dylan nodded. ''One person.''

''Quade's my one person. He's a thinker, not a fighter.'' The old man laughed again. ''He's not my hired muscle. I pay people for what I want. I pay for the land. Now, if the landowner influences the opposition to my project... Well, that's something I can't be held accountable for.''

Dylan grappled for a maneuver, then decided on the truth. ''I'm working on who you've optioned this land from. The estate doesn't publicly list the beneficiary because the property is in a trust. I have the district attorney working on a subpoena.''

The wrinkled hands steepled together on the polished desktop. ''You want to know?''

''Do you know?'' Dylan's pulse quickened. The trustee had the most to lose if Chet Oliver's opposition stopped the mall.

A smile spread across the old man's face, a flash of white in the shadows. ''Quade's working on it, too. This trustee is quite determined to remain anonymous. Wonder why.''

Noise erupted in the hall. ''Dylan!'' Lindsey's voice rang out in urgency.

Dylan threw open the French doors and stopped dead. Lindsey grasped the silk sleeve of another woman's blouse. ''Look, Dylan!''

"What are you doing?" He should have handcuffed her.

"It's her. Sarah Mars."

"I'm Sarah Hutchins. Let go of me!" Hatred flashed in her gray eyes when she swung her gaze to Dylan.

"She just came in...." Lindsey let go of the woman and stepped back.

"Mommy!" A young boy bounded down the stairs and into the marble foyer. His golden hair glinted under the chandelier. "I'm glad you're home."

Dylan's stomach pitched, and his knees started to shake. He turned to Lindsey. "The other rumors... About her, Steve's sister."

Lindsey's cold fingers slid over his hand. "Some rumors are true, then."

The albums had been destroyed in the fire, but Dylan remembered photos of himself and Jimmy at that age—nine going on ten. All arms and legs and tousled blond hair.

"You're wrong!" Sarah's face flooded with mottled red. "I know what you're thinking, and you're wrong." She grabbed her son and tugged him into the library with her.

"Sarah." Robert Hutchins sighed, defeated. He flipped on the lamp near his desk, light washing over his face and the cane propped against his chair.

"Sarah, why not tell me?" Dylan reached out to touch the boy, but Sarah stepped between them. Through his mind flashed a memory of a woman in Detroit stepping in front of her child, taking a bullet for a drug deal gone bad. That child had lacked the innocence of Jimmy's son, but his mother had loved him enough to sacrifice her life for his. He suspected the same was true of Sarah Hutchins.

The boy slipped from her grasp and vaulted around the desk to Robert Hutchins.

Sarah hissed under her breath. "After what you did to my brother, you think I'd let you near my son? Leave. Now."

"Steve did that to himself." But somehow he should have prevented it. Familiar guilt washed over him.

"Liar. All you Matthewses are no good. Your brother took advantage of my teenage crush on him. He used me." Her eyes flashed again, hatred blazing at him. "My son is a Hutchins."

The boy skipped back to his mother. "I'm Jeremy Hutchins." He held out a hand to Dylan.

Before Sarah could intervene, Dylan took the thin hand. "Deputy Dylan Matthews, Jeremy. Pleased to meet you." His voice cracked.

"A cop? A real cop? Do you have a gun and everything? Did you bring your car here? Can I work the siren? I want to be a cop, too. I have a badge and everything." The questions had been fired without a breath.

Dylan had fired those same questions at Sheriff Buck when he'd been Jeremy's age. "I didn't bring the car or the gun today. I have my badge, though."

Sarah trembled. "Jeremy, you're supposed to be in bed."

"I want to see his badge. He's a real cop." The boy raised his chin in defiance.

Dylan flipped out his wallet and pulled the badge from it. "Usually it's on my uniform, but I'm off duty now."

The boy ran his finger over the shiny metal. "You have a number and everything. I'm going to have a real one, too, someday. Aren't I, Dad?"

In the light, Hutchins was an old man. He sighed. "I believe you will, son. You'll be anything you want to be."

"Now, Jeremy!" Sarah pointed toward the door. "Bed."

"Are you a cop, too?" Jeremy turned to Lindsey, the first twinkling of male appreciation of female beauty glinting in his deep blue eyes. He was Jimmy's son, all right.

"Naw, I'm a reporter." Lindsey smiled. "I write stories for the newspaper."

The kid ran his finger over Dylan's badge again. "I wish you'd brought the car and the gun." He expelled a wistful sigh.

Sarah propelled her son from the room. At the door he caught the jamb and turned back. "It was nice meeting you, Deputy Matthews."

"You, too." With a trembling hand Dylan shoved his badge in the front pocket of his jeans. His heart hurt. Lindsey's cold fingers slid around his and squeezed.

"Sit down before you fall down." Hutchins gestured toward a chair before his desk.

Dylan sank into it, stunned. He'd thought himself totally alone, no family left. But there was Jeremy.

"She's not going to let you see him again." The

old man leaned his head against the back of his chair. "I have money, lawyers. On your paltry salary, you can't challenge me."

"He's my nephew."

"He's my son." The old man's voice broke.

Lindsey huffed out a breath. "This is ridiculous. Dylan was not involved in Steve's death. He doesn't deserve to be treated like a criminal—"

"As my brother was treated." Sarah strode back into the room. "He was handcuffed, convicted and executed—"

"He hung himself!" Lindsey defended.

"He was innocent."

"He confessed." Dylan sighed.

Sarah shook her head, tumbling auburn hair around her shoulders. "That lawyer advised him to plead guilty, to save his family the ordeal of a trial he'd lose, anyway."

"That lawyer is dead." Lindsey's dark eyes narrowed.

"I know, and I'm glad."

"Sarah!" Hutchins cautioned. "You've said enough. Calm down. This isn't doing you any good."

"We know where you were, Mr. Hutchins, on the night Oliver died. Quade vouched for you." Lindsey turned back to Sarah. "But where were you?"

"Get out of my house!" Sarah shrieked.

Dylan forced his weight on his trembling legs and tugged on Lindsey's hand. "We're leaving."

"But, Dylan…" Lindsey protested.

"Not now." His gaze fell on Sarah's livid face.

Her rage had twisted her pleasant features into ugliness. He shook his head.

In the driveway he sat behind the wheel of the Expedition and gazed for a long moment at the house. His nephew lived in this mansion. What could he offer a boy who had everything?

The badge in his pocket bit into the flesh of his thigh. The boy had been fascinated by it.

"Another time," he promised. Then he turned the key in the ignition. "And I'll bring the squad car next time."

He caught Lindsey's smile and her soft agreement. "He'd love that."

THE FOG SWALLOWED DYLAN as he strode away from the motel room Lindsey had rented. "You're going to be okay?" she called after him.

His golden blond head bobbed once, and his voice drifted back to her. "I need to walk awhile."

"Don't get hit by a car. There's no visibility out here now." That had been her argument for him to stop the vehicle and stay in Traverse City. She hadn't had to argue very strenuously.

He'd been too stunned by the discovery of his nephew to fight the elements. Would he figure out he couldn't fight the Hutchinses, either?

"Yes, Mother," he called over his shoulder.

She stepped back into the motel room and closed the door. A chair was crammed into the crowded double room next to the window. She sat on it and jerked up the blinds to watch for Dylan's return. Then she flipped open her cell phone.

"Dad," she said when he gruffly answered. "Dylan and I have stopped for the night in Traverse. The fog's just too thick to drive on."

"Marge told me you two were probably headed there," he said.

She recognized his tone. "Fishing, Dad? I'm a reporter working on a story. That's all."

"Is it, honey? You had a lot of feelings for Dylan Matthews when you were younger."

"That's it, Dad. When I was young. I'm not young anymore."

He chuckled. "To me, brat, you're just a baby. I'm glad you're not trying to drive in this soup, but I'm worried about you, anyway."

"It's nothing, Dad."

"You're not sharing the same room?"

"You're not asking that question. Are you alone now?" she snapped. An image of him and Marge together like the night she'd caught them on her living room couch rolled through her mind. Her heart ached with the memory.

"Lindsey."

"Yeah, that's what I thought. Let's just leave it, okay? I'm at the Grand Traverse Motor Lodge if you need me, all right?"

"You're thinking about your mother."

"At least one of us is."

Silence.

She dragged a shaky hand through her messed-up curls. "I'm sorry, Dad. I've never done enough for her. I am a brat."

"Lindsey, you've always been too hard on yourself. You take care, okay?"

"Yeah. We discovered something pretty shocking here, Dad."

"What?"

"It'll keep until we get back. You take care, too." With a soft click, she cut the connection.

Then she dialed the Winter Falls police department. From almost a year of bothering Dylan there, she'd committed the number to memory. "This is Lindsey Warner, forward my call to the sheriff, please."

A few clicks later Sheriff Buck's loud voice boomed in her ear. "Yeah, girl, Dylan all right?"

She smiled at his gruff concern. Then, remembering the way Dylan had walked off into the fog, her smile faded. "Well, he's out walking. He had quite a surprise here, Sheriff. We're in Traverse, holed up in the Grand Traverse Motor Lodge due to the fog."

"It's nasty out," he agreed. "What was his surprise? Or is that personal?"

She laughed. "It has nothing to do with me. But I'll let him tell you when we get back."

"He's out walking? He did a lot of that after his mother died and then after his father. He tries to get ahead of the pain."

The sheriff's insight had her mouth falling open.

"I know the boy, Lindsey. Known him his whole life. He's a good boy."

It was the opening she needed. She'd been burned in the trust department, too. And she'd done a lot of growing up. "You never thought he had anything to do with Steve Mars's suicide?"

Silence.

"I know you never pressed charges—"

"I wouldn't. Dylan is an exemplary officer. He came on duty after Steve Mars had already been put back in the holding cell after his sentencing. I never thought it. Neither did you."

Then. She didn't say it, though. "No, it's just that it came up tonight."

"Dylan talked about it?"

"No." She sighed. "Someone else did." Her battery beeped low. "I've gotta let you go, Sheriff. We'll be back in the morning."

"Take care and wait till the fog's cleared some before you head out."

"We will," she promised, and flipped her phone shut.

The fog had thickened outside the window. Concern for Dylan brought moisture to her eyes. She closed the blinds and walked into the bathroom to splash some water on her face.

She feared it would be a long night. How far would Dylan have to walk to outrun the pain of never knowing his nephew, or really even knowing his brother?

Chapter Six

A short while later Lindsey stepped out of the bathroom and jumped at Dylan's sudden reappearance. He reclined on one of the double beds in the motel room. His eyes were closed, but the jerky rise and fall of his chest suggested he wasn't asleep.

"You're back?"

He didn't answer the ridiculous question.

"I called the sheriff and Dad, so they wouldn't worry. They were glad we'd stopped because of the fog."

"Did I know him at all?" He rubbed his hand over his stomach.

Lindsey sat on the bed next to his. The hotel room was small, the beds no more than a foot apart. But it was clean, and it wasn't in Winter Falls. After his recent surprise, Dylan couldn't have handled the intensity of the memories in Winter Falls.

"Jimmy?" She dragged in a deep breath. "He was a lot of fun, always out for a good time."

"I envied him that." Dylan ran his hands over his face. "I need a shower."

"You're not going to just wash this away." Lindsey reached a hand across the space between the beds and patted his broad shoulder.

He groaned. "She was sixteen. He was twenty-three. I can't believe…" He trailed off miserably.

"But you do. And you blame yourself for not putting a stop to it."

"He kept saying I should take you up on your offer. I thought he was joking."

"You'd hoped." She shivered. If Dylan had been less honorable, she could have been like Sarah, a teenage mother.…

Abruptly he swung his legs over the bed, so they shared the space with hers, knee brushing against knee. "Did he try anything with you?"

Lindsey winced over the despair in his deep voice. "No, not really."

He caught her chin in his hand and tilted it, so her eyes were level with his. "He did?"

"He was just being Jimmy. He never forced anybody. Sarah had a crush on him, like I had on you. But Jimmy wasn't half the man you are."

The deep blue of his eyes shifted, rage flashing. "She was his best friend's little sister. How could he?"

Lindsey shook her head, her curls wrapping around his wrist where his hand still held her face. "I don't know." She sighed. "So that's why Steve killed him."

Dylan shrugged. "I always wondered about that. It didn't seem right. Steve was Jimmy's best friend. I envied them their closeness. Then Steve killed him."

Lindsey's heart ached for the pain in his voice and

on his handsome face. "We don't need to talk about this. It happened a decade ago."

"A reporter who doesn't want to talk something to death?" His hand slipped from her face.

"You've had a shock today. You don't need to talk about Jimmy now."

He chuckled, bitterness giving it an edge. "I have a nephew I never knew. And if Sarah has her way, I won't get to know him."

"She wasn't talking rationally. It was a shock for Sarah to see you."

"Was it? Why'd she come back to Winter Falls after all these years?"

"She didn't, Dylan. We're miles from Winter Falls." She gestured with wide arms.

"But her husband's mall won't be. And didn't you say the bartender told you their move here was recent?"

She nodded, and her reporter's mind started with questions. "Why?" Lindsey asked.

Her practical sense provided some answers. "After her parents adopted Steve from Arborview, they stayed in Winter Falls. They believed it was a great small town in which to raise children. Maybe Sarah believes the same, so she moved close to it. You've been gone a long time, Dylan. She couldn't have known you'd return. No one thought you would."

"Because they thought I killed Steve Mars." The bitterness choked his voice. He cleared his throat. "Thank you."

"For what?"

"For defending me. Thank you for saying that I didn't, that I couldn't."

A wave of nausea washed over Lindsey, and she wiped her sweaty palms on the denim covering her knees. "Yeah, I had your back at Hutchins's."

Dylan's hand covered hers over her knee and squeezed. "I like you having my back."

"Ten years ago I defended you, after you left. I yelled at the gossips, told them they were wrong." She remembered the vigor of her defense, her blind love and trust for a man she'd never really known. She'd been so young and trusting. But she wasn't anymore.

"You shouldn't have done that. You didn't have to. I was gone."

"And I blamed them for driving you away. Then I blamed them for pitying me after my mother, well…"

His hands slid up her arms to her shoulders. He leaned close, so that his lips brushed hers. Soft. Fleeting. Sweet.

She would have accused him of pity, too, but then he deepened the kiss. Hard. Lingering. Hot. His mouth slid over hers, pushed and pulled until their tongues mated. He urged her closer.

Lindsey's heart hammered in her chest. She'd bet Dylan could count its beats. His kiss was warm and passionate, all the things rumor claimed he wasn't. And full of gratitude for her defense of him.

She dragged her mouth from the temptation of his. "No, you shouldn't be thanking me," she managed to gasp.

"What?" He stared at her, his blue eyes glazed with desire. She'd never believed he could feel that for her. But he didn't know the whole truth.

"Ten years ago, I truly believed you couldn't harm anyone for any reason. But I've seen a lot since then. I know that good, rational people are moved to do horrible things. Some for no reason. You believed you had a reason."

Dylan swung his legs over hers and struggled through the small space between the beds. He stopped at the window. The blinds were pulled. She didn't know what he could be looking at, just that he couldn't look at her.

"So," he said, still facing the window, "it'd be okay if I killed Steve Mars because I believed I had a reason?"

Lindsey shivered at the coldness of his tone. "I didn't say that. No, it wouldn't."

"I don't think so, either. And I think you still believe in me, Lindsey. It's yourself you doubt." He turned back to her, his eyes penetrating.

Lindsey shivered again at the heat in his gaze. "Yeah, maybe I do. But this…" She lifted a hand to encompass the small motel room. "This shared room was because there was only one vacancy. The fog drove many travelers off the road. The lot's full of big rigs. I wasn't—"

"It's okay, Lindsey. I know you're a tease, just all talk."

She would have blustered and taken offense, but he smiled as he laid down the insult. She narrowed her eyes, but she wouldn't call his bluff because he'd already called hers.

"I'm going to take a shower." He exhaled a gusty sigh. "A cold one."

Lindsey forced her wicked chuckle. "Want me to wash your back?"

"There you go again."

On his way around the beds to the bathroom, he paused behind her and squeezed her shoulder. "Who's this guy who hurt you, Lindsey?"

She shrugged, but his hand remained. "Nobody. But at one time I thought he was somebody. I was wrong. That hurt more than anything he did."

He tugged a curl, and she hissed a curse at him even as her lips curved into a smile. "Pride," he scoffed.

She laughed. "And you always thought I had none."

"No, that was just a rumor. I never believed it."

DYLAN LINGERED in the shower, shivering under the tepid drizzle from the bent showerhead. He had to contort his neck to get his hair wet, but he stayed behind the locked bathroom door. He'd caught Lindsey's naughty little chuckle when he'd turned the lock.

Then she'd called out, "Didn't you just accuse me of being all talk?"

"Well, you've done some peeping, too."

"Shy?" she taunted. "You have no reason to be."

His shower had started icy cold. He finished with one blast of warm before he shut off the faucet.

Her voice drifted through the door. "You don't mind staying here?"

With her? He heard the unspoken part of her question. But he did mind staying with her. Kissing her had been a major mistake. He wanted her. He wanted the incessantly questioning Lindsey Warner.

"No," he said. "I know we're about a half hour from Winter Falls, but it wouldn't have been smart driving in this thick fog."

"Not used to it anymore?" she asked through the door while he toweled off.

"Detroit has fog, too. But it does get thick here." He might have forged on over her suggestion to stop if he hadn't been so stunned by what they'd discovered in the Hutchinses' home.

"You were distracted," she added.

He sighed as he stepped into his jeans. He left the shirt on the bathroom counter as he opened the door. "Yes. Any ideas?"

"Hmm?" she murmured as she glanced up at him. She reclined on her back on the bed, which immediately brought to his mind the image of lying on top of her.

He swallowed a groan and leaned against the bathroom doorjamb. "Uh," he stammered, trying to remember what he'd asked her.

"Any ideas about what?" she prompted.

"My nephew. How to get visiting—"

From the corner of his eye, he glimpsed a shadow behind the blinds. Instinct had him diving for Lindsey just as the first gunshots rang out.

He rolled with her into the foot of space between

the beds and pressed her face into his chest. His heart jumped with an erratic beat against the softness of her mouth.

A bullet shattered the window.

"You're okay?" he whispered as glass rained onto the floor on the other side of the bed.

She jerkily nodded, her lips brushing against his bare chest.

"Damn it, I never would have gone anywhere in Detroit without my gun." He cursed his stupidity. "I didn't think I'd need it today." Even while he spoke, his mind played with images of the shooter bursting into the room.

He had to protect Lindsey. He had to act. Before he could, the gunshots stopped and footsteps retreated from outside the room.

He vaulted over the bed and to the door, but the fog enveloped the vehicle careening out of the lot. Other guests nervously peered from around cracked open doors as Dylan stood outside the shot-up motel room.

"I called 911," Lindsey said from behind him. He admired the evenness of her voice while her face was stark with fear. He pulled her under his arm and absorbed her trembling.

"Did anybody see anything?" he asked, as he pulled his badge from his wallet with his free hand. "I'm a deputy with the Winter Falls Police Department."

"A big car just tore out of here."

Someone walking up from the lot added, "I think it was white."

An image rolled through his head. A white Lincoln in Hutchins's driveway.

"Anybody see the shooter?"

"Too scared to look out."

He nodded, glad they'd stayed safe. He'd hate to endanger anyone else with his investigation. Before the Traverse police pulled into the lot with their lights bouncing around the fog, he'd discovered all there was to learn.

"IT'S NOT MARGE'S DINER," Dylan said as he slid back into the booth across from Lindsey.

The diner didn't impress her, either. But at least its windows were intact. No sleep and too much coffee had made her cranky. She smacked the table in front of his plate of congealed eggs.

"Damn it, Dylan, why can't you see it? Someone's trying to kill us—either one of us or both of us. These are not accidents. That gun didn't accidentally shoot out the motel room window."

He stuck his fork into the yolk of his eggs, and she thought yellow dust came out. "I'm not saying it was an accident. I'm saying we have no proof to make accusations. Those shots could have been intended for the couple next door to our room. They were married but not to each other."

Lindsey ran her fingers through her wild hair and wished she'd taken a shower before they'd left the crime scene. "And the fire?"

"Mr. Smithers admitted—"

"Admitted to pouring gasoline all around your

house to start his leaves burning the night before? I don't think so. Why are you being so stupid?''

A flash of anger glinted in his red-rimmed eyes. ''Why are you being so paranoid? What's the motive for killing either of us?''

''Revenge,'' she instantly supplied. She remembered the irrational rage that had twisted Sarah Hutchins's face when the woman had glared at Dylan.

He sighed heavily and pushed his plate to the end of the table. ''Proof, Lindsey. You go making accusations to a man like Robert Hutchins, and you'll be the defendant in a courtroom.''

''You're scared of him, of his power?'' she taunted.

''Leery. You're a reporter. You know what power buys.'' He dropped his gaze to the cup of coffee in front of him.

Lindsey jumped up and grabbed the pot from behind the counter. The waitress slept on a magazine at the other end of it. Lindsey splashed some more thick black brew in both their cups.

''I'm mad,'' she said when she slid back into the booth. ''I don't like this. I didn't come home to be burned up or shot at. I came home to get away from all that. I wanted the peace and quiet we always had in Winter Falls.''

Dylan laughed. He laughed so hard, he bent over on his booth and held his stomach. ''Yeah, me too. Peace and quiet. God, I'm tired.''

Lindsey leaned against the wall of the diner and propped her feet on the torn vinyl booth. A few tears slipped down her cheeks, too, but they weren't from laughter.

"Peace and quiet," she repeated into the eerie silence of the all-night diner.

"Yeah. So you think I'm stupid?" he asked over the rim of his coffee cup.

She glimpsed tenderness in his eyes just before he reached over and brushed the tears from her cheeks. "Yeah, you're stupid," she said on a tremulous breath.

His smile just managed to tug up the corners of his mouth. "I don't want you involved in this anymore, Lindsey. Let me handle this alone."

"I can help you, Dylan." The zing of discovery whipped through her, energizing her. "We're close to finding out who killed Chet."

Dylan shook his head and rumpled his blond hair with agitated hands. She envied him the shower he'd taken earlier. "I don't want your help, Lindsey."

Lindsey growled out her frustration. "What is your problem?" She smacked the scratched table again. A glance at the waitress confirmed the woman didn't even stir from her slumber.

Dylan sprawled in his booth, his arm along the back of it. "I told you. I don't trust reporters."

She scrutinized him carefully. His jaw tensed, a muscle jumped in his cheek, and rage simmered in his deep blue eyes.

She laughed now. "You're protecting me? Oh, my, you're protecting me!"

"I'm no good at protecting people, Lindsey. That's why I can't have you around."

She sprang up from her seat, grabbed his handsome face in both hands and dropped a smacking kiss on his tight mouth. ''You saved my life twice now, Dylan. You are my hero!'' She settled back onto the creaking plastic.

''Leave it alone, Lindsey,'' he ground out. His blue irises gleamed within the red veins running through his eyes.

''I love it! You're protecting me. So who do you suspect? Tell me, tell me.''

Dylan snorted. ''Some professional interview. Tell me. Tell me,'' he mocked. He tossed some bills on the table and stood up. He shrugged into the leather bomber jacket he'd earlier dropped onto the empty seat behind him.

''So tell me,'' she insisted, and sidled out of the booth and into the crook of his arm. She loved how naturally he closed his arm around her. She sighed and fought the urge to swoon. She had to say it again, ''You were protecting me. Nobody's ever done that but Dad.''

''I know why.'' He groaned. ''Come on. Dawn's burning off the fog.''

''Don't mention burning.'' She shivered as she matched his long stride to the Expedition parked outside.

He opened her door, leaned her against it and took her mouth. She offered it freely and then hungrily demanded more. He tasted of stale coffee and charred toast, and she'd never enjoyed a flavor more.

His lips slid over hers, and his tongue penetrated with long, sensuous strokes. Under his thin veneer of gentleness, she could feel the passion simmering in him. Hers rose to match his. Her fingers twined into his soft hair and pulled him closer.

"I want more, Dylan," she whispered. "I don't want just talk anymore."

His mouth trailed across her cheek to her ear. "You pick a fine time to tell me that. We have no motel room, and we have to get home. Come on." Effortlessly he lifted her into the passenger's seat.

Lindsey's backbone dissolved as she melted into the soft leather. "Dylan."

"Later. We will. I promised myself there'd be a later for us."

Her lips curved into what she was sure was an idiotic smile. "Later, then."

ON THEIR WAY OUT OF TOWN, Dylan drove past the Hutchinses' estate. If only he could see his nephew again....

He slowed the SUV and stared at the wrought-iron gate. Without trying the security intercom, he knew he'd not be getting through those gates again without a search warrant.

Lindsey's cold fingers pressed his over the steering wheel and squeezed.

"Your hands are always so cold." He turned his hand over to entwine his fingers with hers. "So that's one true rumor—cold hands, warm heart."

She snorted. "Not at all. Don't you know? Most rumors aren't true. Sometimes I wonder if I have a heart anymore."

She smiled over her lightly spoken words, but he glimpsed sadness in her dark eyes.

"You have a heart, Lindsey."

She shook her head, tossing the curls around her slumped shoulders. "You don't know me."

Although she tried to pull her hand away, he held tight. "That was true ten years ago, Lindsey. But not now. We've been through a couple of tough situations. I know you now." He lifted her hand to his mouth and pressed a light kiss against her knuckles.

She closed her eyes.

"Let me take you home," he said. "You're already half asleep."

"We have to talk to them, find out if they were behind last night's shooting."

Dylan gestured to the Traverse City police cruiser parked in a neighbor's driveway. "This isn't my jurisdiction, nor your concern. It's being checked out."

"Someone's trying to kill me." Her dark eyes burned in her ashen face. "That makes it my concern."

"No, that's the company you're keeping." And he had to put some distance between them. For her safety...

Later would have to be much, much later.

Chapter Seven

Lindsey had abandoned her search for gossip. All she sought at Marge's Diner that late morning was caffeine and sugar.

"You look like hell, sweetie," the blond proprietress told her as she flipped over Lindsey's cup and filled it with dark coffee.

"Cinnamon roll," Lindsey croaked, her voice rusty.

Dylan had dropped her at Marge's and continued on to the police station. He'd wanted to drop her home, but she'd left her substitute vehicle in Marge's lot.

As uneasy as driving her mother's car made her, she had to have the freedom of her own transportation. Despite his orders to stay out of it, Lindsey had an investigation to conduct.

"Sure thing." But the petite Marge didn't hustle off to fill her order. She propped a hand on her trim hip and stared down at Lindsey.

Lindsey stared back. She was aware her hair looked as if she'd styled it with an eggbeater. Her eyes blurred from lack of sleep. But she suspected Marge looked deeper.

"What?" Lindsey snapped.

"Did you get what you wanted?" the older woman finally asked.

Lindsey squeezed her eyes shut and could actually hear the rasp of her swollen eyelids against her dry eyeballs. "I don't know what you're talking about."

She blinked her eyes open to witness Marge sliding into the seat across from her. The diner owner lowered her voice to a whisper. "Dylan?"

Lindsey chortled and reached for her cup. "Subtle, Marge. Are you my best girlfriend now? You think I'm giving you any details?"

"You really hate me." Marge sighed and tucked a strand of bleached hair behind her ear.

Lindsey studied the fine lines in the other woman's face. They fanned from her eyes and her mouth. Laugh lines. She didn't remember her mother ever laughing.

"No, not now. Maybe when I was a teenager and found out about you and my dad. Yeah, I did then. But that feels like a hundred years ago."

"So you're saying your feelings have changed?" Marge pursued.

Lindsey hoped the older woman hadn't woven dreams around her father. In all the unhappy years of his marriage, William Warner had never considered divorcing Retha. That Lindsey knew was true. But there wasn't much else of which she could be certain.

She actually reached across the table and squeezed Marge's hand. Then she stared at her appendage as if it had acted of its own accord. Shaking her head, she said, "Yeah, I guess they have."

"I'm glad," Marge whispered, and Lindsey could hear the emotion behind her words.

"And for Dylan? Did your feelings change for him, too?" The older woman's eyes widened with the question.

Lindsey shrugged. "I don't trust my feelings anymore, Marge."

"You went so far from home to get your heart broken, Lindsey."

"Chicago isn't so far, but my heart was broken before I ever left home."

"I'm sorry."

Lindsey nodded, but Marge's sympathy made her edgy. She took a quick swallow of coffee. "You had the wanderlust once, didn't you?"

"What?"

"Rumor has it, you were a foreign exchange student your last year of high school. That's the reason for the crepes on the menu, right?"

Marge laughed as she slid out of the booth and rose to her feet. "That's ancient history."

"Must have been quite an adventure. But you came home, too."

"There's no place like home." Marge chuckled as she walked away.

Since she'd been home, there'd been a murder, her mother had escaped the sanatorium, and a fire and shooting had nearly taken her life.

"Yeah," she whispered. "There's no place like home."

She'd just finished her enormous cinnamon roll when Dylan and the sheriff stepped into the diner. Dylan had showered again, damn him, and changed into his uniform. But she could see him so clearly without it.

She nearly choked on her sip of coffee.

"Lindsey," the two men greeted her.

She narrowed her eyes at the way they stood before her booth. At Marge's nobody stayed on their feet unless there wasn't a free seat. The sheriff couldn't meet her eyes, and Dylan wore his dark glasses.

"What!" she gasped. Her head pounded and her eyes burned from lack of sleep. "I really can't handle anything else right now."

"The sanatorium just notified us, Lindsey. Your mother's been missing since sometime last night."

She squeezed shut her tired eyes and cursed away the sting of threatening tears. "They just notified you? Does my dad know?"

Dylan cleared his throat. "They were hoping they'd find her themselves this time. There's some question of security."

"I guess so." She blew out a ragged breath.

"You kids are dead on your feet." The sheriff awkwardly patted her shoulder. "Why don't you both get some rest? I have other people on this. Your father knows, Lindsey. He's staying at the house, but your mother hasn't shown there yet."

A cold autumn evening had just passed. The fog had dampened the earth. "She's out there alone. Cold. Scared." She shivered as she thought of her mother wandering around, lost in more ways than one.

Dylan slid into the seat beside her and wrapped his arm around her.

"Why now, Dylan?" she asked. All she saw in his eyes were twin reflections of her own bedraggled self.

He shook his head.

"Marge," Lindsey called out, but she didn't have to call far.

Marge hovered behind the sheriff.

"She's been in there nine years. Has she ever escaped before?"

Marge shook her head. "She always seemed content there."

"You visited her?" Lindsey gasped over the pressure of guilt lying heavy on her heart.

Marge nodded. "At least once a month. She seemed fine, honey."

Lindsey hadn't seen her mother in so long, but her father's mistress had visited her once a month. The cinnamon roll tangled around her guts and tried to rise with the guilt. "Yeah. Okay. Thank you."

She pushed against Dylan's side, making him slide back across the vinyl until he stood and helped her from the booth. "I have to—"

"You're asleep on your feet."

"I slept on the way home."

"Twenty minutes, and I doubt that. You complained about my driving enough to indicate you weren't sleeping at all." Dylan slid a gentle finger down her cheek.

She fought a laugh, knowing it would become hysterical.

The sheriff's bellow of advice echoed in the nearly empty diner. "Take her to my house, Dylan. She—"

"No, I'm going home," she argued.

"I'll drop you off," Dylan insisted. Before she could open her mouth with her protest, he finished, "Someone will bring your car by later."

"What car?" Marge asked. "Your Jeep burned."

"My mother's car. The old white Bonneville," Lindsey said, waving a hand in the general direction of the parking lot. The effort made her dizzy.

Marge shook her head. "If you left it there yesterday, it's gone. The lot was empty this morning."

"Oh, okay. Now my car's been stolen." Her knees threatened to give, but she locked them.

The sheriff rubbed his stubbled chin. "I can't believe it. What's happening to this town?"

In Lindsey's tired mind, he acted more concerned about a stolen vehicle than a murder. What had he done to find Chet Oliver's killer? Whatever she and Dylan had done, and she wasn't sure what they'd accomplished, they'd brought on a vicious attack.

Lindsey threw the back door of the diner open then staggered out. She reeled under the glare of the midmorning sun, glinting off the metal of some vehicles in the parking lot. The Bonneville wasn't parked among them.

"It's not there." Feverishly she retraced her steps of the previous, interminably long day. "I can't believe it."

Dylan's arm came around her again. "Come on. I'll take you home."

DYLAN CLOSED THE DOOR of the office of the director of the Arborview Sanatorium. Not only was Mrs. Warner lost, so were the adoption records from when Arborview operated as a home for unwed mothers.

As he stepped into the hall, he casually noted a man and a woman standing at the end of the corridor. He looked again.

Lindsey. He'd left her with her father. Exhaustion had weakened her arguments and she'd gone calmly into her room while Dylan had talked with William Warner.

She must have sensed his stare because she glanced in his direction. She flashed him an impudent grin. Lying, little tease.

The male nurse's aide gave her one last, longing glance before he returned to his duties.

Dylan turned around and headed out the door, giving a cursory nod to the security guard on duty. He strode over to his patrol car, sorely tempted to kick a tire.

The woman drove him insane. She always had, even when she'd been just a girl.

"If I show you mine, will you show me yours?" she called out to him.

He sputtered out a laugh before he could stop it. "All talk, Lindsey. You're all talk."

"My talking got some information. How about yours?"

He turned toward her. Dark circles underlined her big eyes. She had showered. Her curls were still damp and unruly. Her face was pale but for two bright spots of color on her cheekbones.

He caught himself reaching out, brushing a knuckle along her jaw. "You're dead on your feet, and you keep pushing yourself."

She swayed but propped a hiking boot on the bumper of his car. "I'm okay." She lifted her chin. "What'd you learn, Dylan?"

He had to smile. Nothing ever dimmed Lindsey's indomitable spirit. "Last night's security guard left his shift early, hasn't shown today."

"Yup. Bought an expensive car last week. Something strange going on," she said, her brow furrowed.

Dylan shook his head. "He probably got an inheritance from an aunt or grandparent. He probably doesn't need to work anymore, so he's not concerned about his job. Got lax. Your mother slipped out."

She snorted.

"Not everything's a conspiracy, Lindsey," he calmly pointed out. He was aware of how much his calmness irritated her.

"Dang but aren't you the eternal optimist? Doesn't play, Dylan. You're a tough, cynical Detroit narcotics officer. Stop trying to protect me. It's not cute anymore." She dragged her boot from the bumper and stomped it on the leaf-strewn pavement.

"I'm a Winter Falls deputy," Dylan corrected her. If he made her mad, she'd get fired up enough that she wouldn't fall on her face from exhaustion.

"Yeah," she agreed. "A deputy, not a bodyguard."

He nodded. "You're right. I've brought you into two dangerous situations now. You're lucky to be alive."

His stomach dipped with the gruesome thoughts he'd not allowed himself during the fire or the shooting. He could have let her down, as he'd let down his family. He could have lost her as he had them. Then he reminded himself he'd never had her.

She slammed her hand into his shoulder. "You idiot!"

Although she was small, her blow left his shoulder stinging. He rubbed his hand over the sore spot. "What was that for?"

"You are not responsible for any of what has happened."

"Really. How do you know that? Half this town thinks I killed Steve Mars because he killed Jimmy. I've been gone ten years. I come back and Steve's lawyer, Oliver, who has something for me, gets murdered. And there have been two attempts on my life!"

He exhaled a ragged breath into the silence following his outburst. Even the birds had stopped chirping in the trees in the near vicinity. He ran shaking hands through his hair.

"Now who's seeing the conspiracies, Dylan?" Lindsey asked after a few tense moments. "And really, why does everything have to be about you?"

He had to shake his head in disbelief. "I just gave you the scoop for your father's paper. I told you what everyone else is probably thinking."

"I never cared what everyone else was thinking."

Lindsey's impudent smile lifted her mouth.

He ran his hands over his face, knocking his dark glasses off and hooking them around his thumb. Before he could put them back on, Lindsey snagged them from his hand.

"But I like knowing what you're thinking, Dylan." Lindsey slipped his glasses into the unruly curls on top of her head.

"And knowing that, you probably think I belong in this place more than your mother does." He gestured behind her to the old brick sanatorium.

He caught her nervous glance over her shoulder. "We'll find her, Lindsey."

"You don't think she's behind the murder anymore?" Fear dimmed the light in her dark eyes.

He shrugged. He wanted someone to blame, so he could stop feeling like his return had caused the murder. But not Lindsey's mother. He didn't want Lindsey to be hurt. "I don't know. We need to find her and find out how she's been getting out. I'm heading now to this guy's apartment."

Lindsey shook her head. "He had a morning flight according to the aide. He's gone."

"Flights were delayed this morning due to the fog. I'll check." He reached into the patrol car for the radio.

Lindsey curled her fingers around his forearm. "Dylan."

He turned to her.

"I don't think you're responsible for any of what's happened."

"That makes one of us." He breathed in her closeness. The seductive scent of freshly blooming roses clung to her.

Lindsey's teasing grin flashed again. "So maybe that's not a given. But I do have some facts, Deputy. I know you're not responsible for me."

"I'm not?" He couldn't keep a heavy heart around her.

She twisted her full lips. "No."

"So you're an independent woman, responsible for yourself?" He had to goad her.

She laughed. "Hell, no. I'm not responsible for me, either."

He dropped the radio and straightened. "You know, you are something else. You look like hell."

"You sweet talker, you," she purred.

He laughed. "You're upset about your mother. You've been in a fire and a shooting, but you never lose your sense of humor."

"This from the stiffest deputy Winter Falls ever had," she scoffed.

"Only around you, Lindsey Warner."

"Ooh," she squealed. "You're loosening up."

"You're good for me," he admitted. But he wasn't for her. He knew it. He'd never been good for anybody.

But he didn't expect her to hang around Winter Falls after her mother was found and the murder solved. She would move on again, as she had all those years ago. As he had. But he'd come home. Now there were only ashes.

SHE'D PROMISED HER FATHER she'd return quickly with his car. She didn't break promises. She'd resisted the temptation of Dylan Matthews and come home.

Although she wrapped her arms around her father's shoulders when she found him alone at the kitchen table, disappointment swamped her. She'd hoped her mother would have found her way home again, as she had the first time.

"I have to go down to the paper, Lindsey. You need some sleep. Why don't you curl up on the living room couch? That way you'd hear the door open...."

"It's okay, Dad. You go ahead."

"Maybe that's not a good idea." He dropped his gaze from hers, and his already pale face drained of what remaining color he'd had.

"Why not?"

He patted her head with a shaking hand. "I'll just stay. You go to bed, get some sleep."

"You need to be at the paper, Dad." Then, as concern clouded his eyes, she added, "What? Why don't you want me to stay here alone?" Her stomach dipped with a sad realization. "You think she's dangerous? You think she might hurt me?"

He sighed heavily. "I don't know. And I don't want to take the chance with you, honey. Come on, now. You're exhausted. Go lie down."

"She wouldn't hurt me, Dad."

He slipped out of her arms as he jumped to his feet. "She almost did. When she set fire to this house nine years ago, she almost killed you then."

"I was at school, Dad." She hated the way her voice broke with the emotion strangling her.

"You came home. You came into a burning house and rescued her. You could have been killed."

A nightmare of wavering flames and overwhelming smoke flashed behind the eyes she squeezed shut. The room spun a bit, and she dropped into the chair he'd vacated.

"I wasn't. She didn't want to hurt me." She twisted her fingers into her tangled curls.

"The other day, the fire at Dylan's—"

"That wasn't her. She never left the sanatorium. She was heavily sedated."

"The shooting last night."

"How'd you know?" Then she answered her own question. "Dylan told you."

He jerked his gray-haired head in a sharp nod. "Yes, someone had to. You wouldn't have told me. You're in danger, Lindsey."

"Both incidents could have been accidents."

"Mr. Smithers burning his leaves, and a jealous husband shooting the wrong motel room," her father agreed. "He said that."

It wasn't what he believed. But it wouldn't stop her from using those theories to protect her father as Dylan had tried to protect her.

"Those are the reasonable explanations. We're in the news game, Dad. We know there are a lot of reasonable explanations..."

He shook his head. "And we know there are unreasonable ones, too."

"Not my mother."

"How do you defend her, Lindsey? I know you're

mad at her, mad at me, at Marge. Why did you come home?''

She folded her arms on the table and dropped her head onto them. ''I don't know, Dad. I hoped you'd want me. Nobody else has.''

She didn't hear his reply because sleep finally won the battle she'd fought against it. The last she knew was the gentle touch of his hand on her hair.

Chapter Eight

Lindsey dreamed of flying, of the weightlessness of being effortlessly lifted and carried along without struggling for every inch of progress.

Then she gently dropped down to the cushion of soft earth, her bag sliding off her shoulder and dropping beside her with a thud. Silk brushed her cheek. New grass? She snuggled into it and recognized her bed from the silk of her pillowcase.

She shivered, but before she could fully acknowledge being cold, her comforter enveloped her shoulders. Sleepily she whispered, "Thanks, Dad."

It wasn't her father's voice that replied in a deep, sexy tone. "You're welcome."

She blinked and stared into the handsome face of Dylan Matthews. "We just keep running into each other." She sighed and ran her finger over the sharp planes of his face.

He turned his mouth to brush a kiss against her fingertips. The softness of his lips and the heat of his breath traveled from the nerves in her fingertips to those in the pit of her quivering stomach.

"How are we running into each other in my bedroom?'' She traced the line of his dark blond brows. ''Am I dreaming?'' But the skin beneath her caressing hand was warm and real. The breath he exhaled into her bangs was hot.

''We met in the kitchen. Your father let me in and asked me to stay. I carried you in here.''

''Ooh,'' she moaned. ''And I was asleep. You'll have to do that again, when I'm awake enough to enjoy it.''

''I carried you before,'' he said. ''At my house. During the fire.'' His deep blue eyes clouded with the memory, and he started to pull away.

Lindsey caught him and wrapped her arms around his neck. ''That doesn't count. I was too terrified to appreciate your strong muscles, your—'' She leaned closer and buried her face in his throat. ''Your delicious smell.''

''You were terrified?'' He wrinkled his brow.

She nodded and slid her lips along the straining cords in his neck. ''Umm-hmm.''

''I'd have never known. You were wisecracking when other people—men and women—would have been crying with fear.'' He trembled in her arms as her lips slid lower and her tongue flicked the jumping pulse in his throat.

''I don't cry as a rule. I always wisecrack when I'm scared.''

''You must be scared all the time,'' he said.

Lindsey feared he was right. ''You haven't found my mother. I know you would have said.''

He shook his head. ''No. And the guard did catch

a flight late this morning, after the fog lifted. We'll catch up with him, Lindsey.''

She didn't want to think it could be too late by then. She didn't want to think at all. She nipped his earlobe and was rewarded with his grunt of pleasurable pain.

''Lindsey…'' His tone threatened.

Threats didn't frighten Lindsey. ''I'm not all talk, Dylan. Let me show you.'' She jerked the tails of his uniform shirt from his perfectly fitting pants. Then she slid her fingers under the crisp cotton and over the ribbed undershirt he wore beneath. ''You're wearing too many clothes, Deputy.''

''Lindsey, your father—''

''Left for the paper, right?''

He nodded and clenched his jaw.

''And he wanted you to stay, to keep an eye on me?''

He nodded again, and his Adam's apple bobbed as he swallowed hard.

''I want more than your eye on me, Dylan. I want your hands, your mouth—''

His mouth obliged, taking hers in a deep, penetrating kiss. But he pulled back to ask, ''Are you sure? Is this right? With everything that's going on?''

She ran a fingertip across his furrowed brow. Always so serious, so earnest, her deputy Dylan. ''I'm not sixteen anymore, Dylan. And when we're in Winter Falls, there will always be stuff going on.''

Her heart flipped with the realization and momentarily dread filled her. But she shoved it away. It had no place in her dream.

Dylan brushed his thumb across her lower lip, and she popped her tongue out to lap at it. He groaned. ''Lindsey, you're not sixteen anymore. I can't ignore you. I don't want to ignore you.''

She laughed as she pulled his buttons free and pushed the khaki uniform shirt from his wide shoulders. Her fingers caressed the bulging muscles of his upper arms. ''That's the idea, Dylan.''

''If you're just teasing me, tell me now. A cold shower may help at this point but not much beyond.'' Even as he warned her, his mouth took hers again in sipping kisses.

Lindsey moaned over the passion of his kiss, of her own response. His lips slid from hers to nip at the edge of her jaw.

''You won't need a cold shower,'' she promised.

Her promise snapped his control. He jerked down the comforter he'd so gently pulled over her moments before.

But the closeness of their clothed bodies as he pressed her into the mattress wasn't enough. Lindsey needed the glide of skin on skin, lubricated by their perspiration.

She pushed against his chest. Dylan released her only long enough to pull her sweater over her head, his knuckles brushing along her bare midriff. His gaze dropped to her chest and her lacy bra.

Because she didn't have much in the way of breasts, she should have felt inadequate. She usually felt inadequate. But the intensity of Dylan's stare and the catch of his breath made her feel beautiful.

She wanted to see him again as she had that day

in his basement. She wanted his chest naked and slick from the perspiration of his passion. She wanted him a little wild and definitely out of control.

Her nails raked up his back underneath the ribbed shirt. "Take it off, Dylan. Now."

Muscles rippling in his arms, he dragged his undershirt over his head. The golden blond waves fell into disarray.

Lindsey flicked her tongue over a flat male nipple.

His fingers tangled in her hair and jerked her mouth to his. Against her lips he groaned and threatened, "You're going to get it for that." But his eyes lit with humor and hunger.

Her pulse tripped madly as his tongue slid in and out of her mouth. His fingers unclasped the lacy excuse for a bra and pushed it from her shoulders. Then his hands cupped her breasts, his fingers tracing the sensitive flesh.

Lindsey captured his tongue, then sucked it deeper. She swallowed his groan and trailed her nails over his sinewy shoulders.

He tore his mouth from hers, panting. "Lindsey," he warned in that too-serious tone that drove her wild.

"Dylan." The husky depths of desire drowned the mockery she'd intended.

He was so beautiful, like a male angel dropped to earth. The afternoon sun slanted through her blinds and glinted in his golden hair and shimmered in his blue eyes. With his sculpted muscles under satin-smooth flesh, he was every woman's secret fantasy.

He pressed a fingertip over her lips as if to stop her from speaking. He needn't have bothered. The power of his masculine beauty had silenced her. Then his slightly rough fingertip trailed from her lips, over her chin, down her throat to her breasts.

Lindsey inhaled a quick breath, which pushed one of her erect nipples closer to his tantalizing finger. He circled the aureole, making her bite her lip to hold back her cry. Then he slowly stroked the hardened nipple.

His mouth took hers again as his fingers stroked her breasts and teased her nipples. Then his tongue followed the trail his finger had taken, down her throat to her breasts. This time, Lindsey couldn't hold back her cry of pleasure.

His tongue flicked and lapped. To hold back another cry, Lindsey nipped his shoulder. "Dylan, I—"

"What, Lindsey?"

"I want more."

She had hardly finished her sentence when he pulled her jeans open and slid his hand inside. But his mouth didn't leave her breasts. As he pushed his fingers inside the lace of her panties, he suckled her.

Lindsey could feel a pull from her nipples to the sensitive spot where the tip of his finger slid inside her. "Dylan!" she screamed as her world exploded.

He groaned. "You're so hot, so wet."

She dug her nails into his shoulders as he drove her up again. "Please, Dylan, please," she panted.

He stared at her face, his eyes a wild blue. His control had snapped. Lindsey's heart raced with the thrill. He jerked her jeans down and stood up to kick off his uniform pants.

Lindsey spread her legs, wanting him inside her.

But instead of covering her, he knelt between her legs and dragged her up to his mouth. Through the lace of her panties, his hot breath penetrated.

With his teeth he dragged the lace down her legs. Then he drove his tongue into her. Lindsey thrashed around on the pillows.

"I can't...I can't..." But she lied. She kept taking everything he gave and still she wanted more.

Contorting her boneless body, she was able to reach him. She stroked the length of his hard, pulsing flesh. "Now!" she ranted.

"Lindsey, I have to protect you," he rasped out. He reached for his pants, knocking her leather bag onto the floor. Then he pulled a packet from his wallet and dropped the wallet onto her bag.

Dylan clenched his teeth as he drove into her. A muscle jumped in his strong jaw. She caught him tight.

He pulled out and then drove back in. "Lindsey, I've never—"

"Oh, you're a virgin?" She writhed beneath him.

He sputtered out a laugh even as he drove her over another edge. She managed to lock her weak legs around his slick back as he pushed her higher and higher.

A sharp keening noise rent the air, and it astounded Lindsey that it emanated from her throat. Her world splintered in flashes of pleasure so intense it was painful. Again and again she came.

Another guttural cry filled the air and Dylan collapsed onto his strong arms, gallantly holding most of his weight from her.

With the convulsing muscles inside, Lindsey pulled him closer.

He groaned again. "You're killing me!"

Lindsey expelled a breath strong enough to stir her bangs, which were sticky with sweat. Then she dragged him closer, welcoming his strong, heavy chest crushing her breasts. She licked his ear and pushed his hair back from his forehead.

"You never what?" The reporter in her had to know.

He chuckled. "I never felt anything like this, never so much. But then, it's you." He rolled to his side, holding her tight in his arms.

Lindsey tucked her head under his strong chin, feeling cherished and protected. "And finally, it's you." She sighed. Her girlish fantasies had been so tame compared to the devastating sensual reality of Dylan Matthews.

Usually she expected too much. Her heart ached over the thought of leaving his arms. The thought became reality as he loosened his hold and slipped from the bed.

Lindsey's mouth fell open, a protest ready. But he touched a finger to her lips.

"I'll be right back." And he swaggered into the bathroom off the bedroom.

She swallowed a sigh over the sight of his dimpled backside and glanced around the room of her adolescence. She'd dreamed many dreams of Dylan Matthews in this room with the faded pink roses and gauzy curtains.

Her room hadn't been damaged in the fire but for

the scent. Special machines had taken care of that, and Marge had offered to help her redecorate. But Retha Warner had chosen those roses for her daughter's room, and Lindsey hadn't wanted to replace them.

Where was her mother now? Was she warm? Was she hungry? Lindsey sighed.

Dylan slid back into bed and took her in his arms. "You okay?"

She nodded, the fear for her mother choking her throat.

He opened his mouth, but before he could speak, she covered his lips with hers.

Breaking away from the swift and sweet kiss, she murmured, "It's all right. I know. This was just this, just the moment."

"Just this? You don't want anything else?" He stroked a finger down her cheek.

Her heart ached with the lie she had to tell. But the last thing she wanted was for him to feel sorry for her. She'd had enough of other people's pity.

"No, what would be the point? Once my mother is found, and I find out whether or not I have a brother, I'll probably leave. Will you stay?"

Dylan gently tipped her head back, and he searched her eyes. But she had no idea for what he searched. "I'll be staying. I don't know why. But I'll be staying."

Lindsey nodded and fought the tears that threatened. He wouldn't have come back for her. He'd never seen her as anything other than a pest.

"You didn't argue with me earlier," she said.

"About?"

"About my mother. You don't believe she and the killer are the same."

Dylan sighed, and Lindsey's heart overflowed with the dread already filling it. "I don't know, Lindsey. Like you, I don't want to think she is."

"Where can she be?" Horrible images of her mother, hurt and alone, flashed through her mind.

Dylan shrugged. "As distracted as you made me, she could be on the other side of the bedroom door. I don't know. I'm working on it. I didn't come here for this—"

"I know that. I threw myself at you again, and this time you caught me. It's okay. I already said I really didn't expect anything from you."

But her foolish heart called her a liar. She'd expected everything from him. But she doubted he had it to give. Because of all the tragedies he'd lived through, he'd locked away his heart long ago. It must have been the only way he'd found to deal with the pain.

"But I expected something from me, Lindsey. I expected to stay focused on your safety."

Lindsey laughed and snuggled closer in his strong arms. "Oh, I wouldn't agree with that. You were pretty focused, Dylan. If you were any more focused, I'd be dead right now."

"That's what I'm worried about."

She glanced into the seriousness in his eyes. He worried about her. Her heart did a crazy little flip. "It's okay. Don't worry. Maybe everything that has happened has been a coincidence, accidents. Nobody wants to harm either of us.''

''I never believed anyone wanted to harm you, Lindsey. I've only thought you were in the wrong place at the wrong time with the wrong man.''

She'd been with the wrong man before, but not this time. Dylan Matthews was the only right man for her. She'd known it when she was sixteen, and she knew it now.

While she had him naked in her bed, she intended to take advantage of it. Later she'd worry about gluing back together her shattered heart.

Her fingers trailed slowly down his side, over his slim hip.

''Lindsey,'' he warned again, but his voice cracked with the threat.

Lindsey didn't heed his warning. She stroked and teased until his breathing grew ragged and his hands restless. He rolled them until she straddled him, and then he reached to the side of the bed, rooting around the items spilled from her purse, for his wallet.

Instead of bringing up a foil packet, he held a velvet jeweler's box in his hand. ''What's this?'' He didn't wait for her answer but popped open the case to reveal the diamond solitaire she'd worn for more than a year.

''Old news.'' She covered his hand with hers and snapped the lid closed.

''You're not still engaged.''

She dropped a kiss on his chest. ''And doing this with you? I'm not that way.''

''But you didn't give it back.''

She shrugged. ''You don't know the rules of etiquette about broken engagements? Guess that's good. You must have never had one. When the man breaks it off, the woman gets to keep the ring. Of course, I tried to give it back, anyway. He didn't want it. His new fiancée, probably wife by now, has a bigger one. I'm going to mail it back.''

Dylan dropped the ring box on the floor and cupped her cheek in his callused palm. ''I want to hurt him, like he hurt you.'' His blue eyes burned.

''I hurt me,'' she corrected him. ''He wasn't the man I wanted him to be.'' She realized that now. She'd wanted him to be Dylan Matthews. It wasn't her ex-fiancé's fault he wasn't.

''You're generous.'' He pulled her down for a deep kiss.

Lindsey gave all, her entire heart, which had been his for more than a decade.

She smiled when he finally eased away. ''No, I'm not. I hope he's miserable with his new honey and that the newspaper fires him. So I'm not generous at all.''

Dylan laughed then, laughed so hard she nearly jiggled off his chest. ''I'll remember that.'' He reached on the floor and pulled a foil packet from the wallet he'd found.

''You do that, Deputy Matthews.''

He threw back his head and groaned as he entered her. ''You're so tight, so perfect, Lindsey.''

''I'll take perfect,'' she murmured, smiling over his lie. Then she began to move, setting a pace, which he matched with a frenzied rhythm.

He took her higher and higher until Lindsey thought she had nothing left to give. Then she gave more. He growled out a victory cry and pulled her tight to his chest.

Lindsey's heart beat in perfect accord with his. Fast. Fast and then slower as the satisfaction put the passion to simmer. She'd never get enough of Dylan Matthews.

"Go to sleep now." He stroked her tangled hair. "You're exhausted."

"Yeah," she sleepily agreed. She relished the safety and security of being held tight in his arms. "You, too. Go to sleep, Dylan."

"I'll hold you while you sleep even though you'd be safer with me gone," he muttered.

She ran a finger over his tense jaw. "You've protected me, Dylan. You've kept me safe from danger."

He snorted. "I've been the danger, Lindsey. Without me, you'd have nothing you'd need protecting from."

She couldn't argue with him there. Without him, she wouldn't have had to protect her foolish heart. She'd already failed miserably at that.

Chapter Nine

Dylan wore his uniform this time. Despite his summons, his visit to Evan Quade's office was official. The summons rankled, though. The businessman's secretary rapped on the door and opened it for Dylan.

Quade faced the windows; his gaze focused on the traffic below him.

"I don't have time to drop everything and run when you or your boss call." Dylan didn't bother keeping the resentment from his voice.

"We've been waiting for you."

"We? Hutchins is here?" Then Dylan noticed the profusion of silky black curls spilling over the back of a leather chair.

"I believe Ms. Warner is your old friend."

Dylan ignored the man and mentally demanded that Lindsey turn around and face him. But then he wasn't eager to face her. He'd slipped out of her rumpled bed sometime last night and hadn't talked to her since. He had no idea what to say.

She'd humbled him with her passion, and she'd introduced him to his own. He'd never wanted like that, had never needed someone as he'd needed her. Desire clawed through his gut. As he still needed her.

"This is an official visit, Quade. I need to ask you some questions. I can't do that with a reporter present."

Quade quirked a brow. "Then I guess the questions will have to wait. I called Ms. Warner here as I believe the press would be interested in knowing who's the trustee of the property Hutchins Enterprises is trying to get rezoned. Did you get your subpoena yet?"

Dylan nodded. "It's in motion now. I should know who the trustee is within the hour."

A mocking smile slid over the businessman's face. "Can you wait that long?"

Dylan bit the inside of his cheek. "You know?"

The dark head nodded. "Money talks."

Lindsey spoke up then. "There's another part to that saying. Do you have proof?"

A smile spread over Dylan's face at her cynicism.

Quade ran a finger down the crease of his suit jacket sleeve. "I have no reason to lie."

"Really." An hour. Could he afford to wait that long? "You could be protecting someone. I want to talk to Sarah."

Quade shook his head. "Not possible."

"I'll get a warrant."

Quade laughed. "What would be your cause?"

Dylan took a step closer to the chair where Lindsey sat. She knew nearly as much about the case as he did. "She's a suspect."

"Mrs. Hutchins?" Quade almost succeeded in sounding shocked.

"Sarah," Lindsey confirmed. "She's quite bitter about the past."

"She was left carrying a dead man's child," Quade ground out. "She has reason to be bitter." He visibly shook himself and straightened his tailored suit. "Of course, the bitterness has passed. She's a happily married woman, wife to one of the most powerful men in the Midwest."

"And mother to my nephew," Dylan added. "Whom she doesn't want me to see. Easiest way to accomplish that would be to permanently get rid of me, like with the gunshots in our motel room after we left her house."

Quade chuckled and waved his hand. "That's not the easiest way. She has legions of lawyers to accomplish that without ever raising her own finger."

"I never said she pulled the trigger herself." Dylan folded his arms over his chest, so he wouldn't reach out a hand for Lindsey's hair. "I've checked you out."

"Did you hear I'm psychic? I would know you two had decided to stay the night when you had only to travel thirty minutes to Winter Falls? And I would know where you'd stay if you stopped due to the fog?"

His patronizing tone made Dylan clench his fists, but Lindsey laughed. "And you'd have us believe you didn't have one of your security guards follow us the minute we'd left your office? You don't think Dylan, with his ten years of police work in Detroit, would miss a tail?"

He fought the smile from his face over Lindsey's

bluff. No one had followed them that night. But he only raised a brow as Quade had earlier.

"Hmm…" Quade's dark eyes held laughter. "Touché, Ms. Warner."

Dylan clenched his fists again and ground his teeth when Lindsey's tinkling laughter rang out. She'd still not turned toward him.

"Lindsey," he said in the threatening tone he used exclusively for her.

She laughed. "So who are you trying to throw suspicion on?"

Merriment danced in Quade's dark eyes. "The person who has the most to gain from the mall project."

"You and Hutchins," Lindsey said.

Quade shook his head. "We're already millionaires, both of us. What's more to us? But millions to a person who's never had them—that's something worth killing for."

"You're saying the person who owns the land you've optioned for the mall?" Lindsey's pen poised over her pad.

Dylan had come to that realization on his own. Only the slow wheels of justice had withheld the identity from him. And now Quade.

"I don't want this in the paper, Lindsey." He stared down Quade.

Lindsey sniffed. "That was our deal. Not yet. Who is it?"

"The sheriff."

"The sheriff owns that much land?" Lindsey asked.

"An inheritance, I believe," Quade confirmed.

''From a grandparent or something. He's been leasing the land to farmers, getting barely enough to cover the taxes on it. If the rezoning goes through, we're talking a lot of money. Sheriff Buck Adams will become a very rich man.''

Dylan's heart beat erratically. ''Money doesn't matter to the sheriff. He's happy with what he has, who he is.'' Dylan had always admired that about the sheriff. His whole life he'd striven to be like him.

''Is he?'' Quade's lips twisted into a smirk.

Lindsey stood up and turned to Dylan. ''He's just needling you, Dylan. There's no reason to believe the sheriff gives a damn one way or the other if the mall deal goes through.''

Dylan nodded, but panic streaked through his guts. Now he knew how Lindsey had felt when she'd learned of her mother's past.

He pushed open the office door and strode out through the reception area. He had to get back to Winter Falls and learn if Evan Quade lied or spoke the horrible truth.

''DYLAN!'' LINDSEY CALLED out as she raced down the sidewalk after his broad back. By the stiffness in his shoulders and the speed of his stride, she knew he was agitated.

He stopped at the curb by his black SUV. But he didn't turn back to her. She could appreciate that. She'd not been ready to face him in Quade's office, either.

She'd completely given herself to this man who didn't want her. But she'd already learned to live with that humiliation. She should have had the guts to face him despite the way he had slipped from her bed last night without a word. No goodbye. No thank you. She had awakened alone.

"Are you okay?" She tentatively laid her hand on his tense arm.

He jerked but didn't pull away. "Yeah, you've got your story now. In a hurry to get back and print it?"

"I'm not printing this story. And I don't know if I can get back to Winter Falls." She squeezed his hard forearm. "I took the bus in and was hoping to catch a ride with you."

"Quade didn't play the gentleman and offer to give you a ride back after your exclusive?" A muscle jumped in his tense jaw.

Lindsey smiled over the bitterness in his tone. Her foolish heart attempted to lift with his show of jealousy. But men were often jealous of each other, and it had nothing to do with the woman.

She'd learned that, too. Her ex-fiancé had been jealous of Dylan even though he'd never cared about her.

She shrugged and admitted the truth. "He doesn't like me much. He'd probably toss me out of the car while it was moving. He just asked me here to rattle you. He thinks you and I are involved."

"Are we?" His gaze dropped to her hand on his arm. "Or was yesterday just an itch you'd had for ten years and finally decided to scratch?"

She laughed. "I should be the one asking that. I wanted you then, and I wanted you yesterday. Today, I don't think so. You're being an ass."

When she would have flounced off, he caught her arm and pulled her close. "I'm sorry," he whispered softly against her lips.

"Sorry for today or yesterday?" She braced her palms against his muscular chest, holding back just enough so that their breaths mingled but their lips didn't touch.

"Both." He groaned. "I shouldn't have left like that, but your father—"

She rose on tiptoe and pressed a kiss against his lips. "You were embarrassed. I'm not sixteen anymore, Dylan. My father doesn't care."

"That's not what he said when we met in the kitchen, but I don't blame him."

"My father talked to you—about what happened?" Now the embarrassment was all hers.

Dylan nodded.

"What did he say?"

"Not to hurt you. You've had enough pain in your life already."

She dropped her head to his chest, her arms hanging limply at her sides. "I'm tough. Did you find my mother?"

"No. We're working on it. I can't believe she could disappear this way."

Lindsey sighed. "But she has. She might be crazy, but she's smart."

"Or she has help."

Lindsey couldn't think about what he might mean. She stroked her fingers along his tense jaw. "Are you okay?"

A ragged sigh blew through his lips. "I don't know."

"Are you going to talk to the sheriff?" She searched his face for signs of his anxiety. He had always idolized the sheriff.

"I have to." His blue eyes glittered.

"You really love him." She skimmed her hands up his arms and squeezed his shoulders.

"He's always been there for me, even before my parents died. He's a good man."

"Rumor is he loved your mother."

"That was true." Dylan leaned his forehead against hers. "He has my mom's picture in his den among all the animal carcasses he's had stuffed. She watches me, too. How can I question him on Chet's murder?"

The anguish in his voice pressed against Lindsey's heart, and she wrapped her arms around his lean torso. "You'll do it because it's your duty." She sighed. "You've always been big on doing your duty."

Dylan tipped her chin back to him and sought her lips. His kiss was long and gentle. Lindsey's knees weakened as her pulse danced around.

When he finally lifted his head, he said in a husky voice, "It's my duty to get you safely back to Winter Falls." He opened the passenger's door for her.

When he slid behind the wheel, he took her hand again. "How are you holding up?"

Her heart clutched. "You mean, about my mother? I don't know. I wasn't really comfortable with her in the sanatorium. I couldn't visit her there. It was too hard to see her like that. She didn't know who I was.

But it worries me that she's alone, that she'll hurt herself or someone else. I really don't think she'd do it purposely," she hastened to add, "but…"

"I know," Dylan said, and squeezed her hand. "I understand."

And he did. He knew her as no other had, and it frightened her. How could he want to keep her when no one else ever had? He who knew her best?

She noted that he didn't promise to find her mother now. With the more time that passed, the harder it became. If she'd had any idea where to search, she would have been beating the bushes herself. But what if he was right, and she'd had help? Who? And why?

But she had never really known her mother. The logical places—Arborview Sanatorium and the house—were being watched. All she could do was wait, and Lindsey didn't do that well.

She needed activity.

As he steered on the road leading back to Winter Falls, Lindsey reached over to run her hand up his thigh.

"Lindsey," he warned.

Twenty minutes later he stopped the truck by the *Gazette*. "Stay with your dad, Lindsey. Stay out of trouble."

She kissed his cheek and squeezed his hand, knowing the ordeal he faced. But she wasn't making any promises.

THE SHERIFF PUSHED OPEN the screen door and stepped inside his house. His pale blue gaze focused on the evidence bag in Dylan's hand and then on Dylan's face.

"You know."

Dylan nodded. "You need to see the search warrant?"

The old man shook his head. "No, I trust you."

Dylan's heart throbbed. He turned back to the den. "I found it."

"What?"

He'd already taken pictures and cataloged what he'd found. He reached for the papers that sat beside his mother's picture on the desk in the same room he'd been sleeping. When he'd been able to sleep...

"Under those scrapbooks you've been keeping on my achievements, I found these. The township maps that Quade went over with Chet Oliver, the alternative sites for the mall. You would have lost millions."

The sheriff rubbed a hand over his stubbled chin. "I don't know what you're talking about, Dylan. I never saw them before."

"Really? They're spattered with blood, probably Chet's. They were on his desk when he was shot. Now they're on yours. What should I believe?" Not the evidence. He did not want to believe the evidence.

His stomach constricted. From all those years ago, his father's words echoed in his ears. "Shut it off, boy. Shut it off!" He had to detach. He had to treat the sheriff as any other suspect.

"Believe in me, as I believed in you, Dylan." The older man sagged onto the sofa bed. He rubbed his hands over his face. "I don't know where those papers came from. You know I never lock the door.

Heck, the whole town knows that. Probably even the newcomers.''

"You mean Quade and Hutchins?"

"They hang around Marge's."

"Why?"

"The food, I guess."

"Not them. You. Why didn't you tell me about the land, about your part in this mall deal?" If he was just an officer interviewing a suspect, why did he feel so betrayed?

The sheriff shrugged. "I'm staying in this town, Dylan. Chet wasn't the only one opposed to the new development. The mayor is, too. And other people, my neighbors and friends. I didn't want them mad at me."

"You're going to become a millionaire but stay here?"

"I lead a simple life, Dylan. I wasn't going to change that." His pale blue gaze traveled to the picture of Dylan's mother. Moisture welled.

"Then why sell the land to them? Why do you want all that money if you're not going to spend it?"

The sheriff pushed himself to his feet. "It wasn't for me."

Dylan's hands trembled in his latex gloves when he slid the documents into the evidence bag. For him. The old man wanted the money for him. "I—I don't know what to say."

"Are you arresting me?"

LINDSEY TAPPED AWAY on her computer keys, then promptly deleted the story. She was too responsible a reporter to write an article on unconfirmed information. But she doubted Dylan would corroborate. She had to wait.

Her dad stepped into the office and dropped a bag on his desk. Dark circles underlined his tired eyes. "Hey, brat. You get anything from Quade this morning?"

She shrugged. "Nothing I can use."

"Want a cinnamon roll?" He reached into the grease-stained bag.

Her stomach pitched. "I'll pass."

"You have to eat something."

"But Mom..."

"They'll find her, Lindsey." He patted her shoulder. "What you working on?"

Shift her mind to work. She had gotten that from her father. "I should go over to City Hall, talk to the mayor. I want his reaction..." She couldn't say it. She'd have to fish, see if the sheriff had put any pressure on the mayor to change his mind about the mall.

"Still feels funny thinking of him as mayor. He used to be the judge."

"That's right." As a reporter, her father had done an excellent job keeping her informed while she'd been away. "An old bachelor judge who retired, then was too bored, so he ran for mayor."

"He was the judge who sentenced Steve Mars." Will Warner sighed. "What a tragedy."

And another line of questions she needed to ask. But first, her father... "Dad, why didn't you mention what Chet said in the diner the day Dylan came back to town?"

He raised his gaze from the grease-stained bag. "About?"

"The letter Steve Mars left for Dylan."

He pushed a hand through his gray hair. "Honestly, brat, I just forgot."

"You forgot?"

He chuckled. "You've been gone awhile, Lindsey. I've gotten old. I forget things."

Lindsey studied the lines in his face. Her father had a lot on his mind. She could forgive his lapse. But she couldn't stop pursuing the story. "I'm heading over to City Hall now."

"The mayor just left Marge's. He was heading home."

She grabbed her leather bag, slinging it over her shoulder. "I'll go there, instead. Where's he live?"

A smile tilted her dad's mouth when he gave her directions. She got as far as the door, then turned around. "Dad, can I use your car?"

He tossed her a key ring. "Use the delivery truck."

She laughed. "You trust me with it?"

"It has a governor on the speedometer. Doesn't go over forty. That's the only vehicle I trust you with."

"Yeah, yeah…"

"Be safe, sweetheart," he called after her.

DYLAN MANEUVERED HIS Expedition onto the mayor's street. Although he wore his uniform, he'd not bothered to get his squad car. He passed a delivery truck for the *Winter Falls Gazette* that was a couple of feet from the curb and pulled into the cement drive of the mayor's brick ranch.

Through his windshield he caught a flash of red and black as Lindsey bounced from foot to foot on the front steps. He pushed open the door and stepped onto the drive.

"Lindsey, what are you doing here?" He'd come to warn the mayor again. He'd already talked to the old man once about his opposition to the mall, and the target his stance had possibly made him. Now he had some questions for the retired judge. And, as usual, Lindsey Warner stood in his way.

"Hey, Deputy!" She wagged her fingers at him and jumped off the steps.

"Lindsey, I told you to stay out of my investigation." He pushed a hand through his hair, exhausted, both physically and emotionally. She'd contributed to both.

"Are you okay, Dylan?"

She smiled at him, her beautiful face soft with understanding. If he had a heart left, he knew he'd give it to her.

He glanced behind her at the brick house just as the world exploded into noise and glass and flying debris. He leaped forward to knock her to the ground, but she'd already fallen and rolled partially under the front of his Expedition.

Her beautiful dark eyes closed, and blood rolled down her cheek from a cut on her forehead. Bits of glass and building had tangled in her curls.

He dropped to his knees in the glass and reached under the bumper for her wrist. Knowing he couldn't move her, he fought the urge to pull her into his arms. He had to leave her where she'd fallen in case she was seriously wounded. With shaking fingers he searched for her pulse.

And then he did something he hadn't done since he'd been a boy trapped in the back seat of a wrecked vehicle watching his mother die. He prayed.

Chapter Ten

The pain rolled around in Lindsey's head like a bowling ball over glass figurines. She figured all her brain matter had shattered. With a groan, she forced open her eyes.

The tilt and sway of the white walls all around her caused the same sensation in her stomach. Had she died and gone to heaven? Even the bright light, a single beam, speared her eyeball.

"She's awake," someone bellowed.

Lindsey winced. "Jeez, take it easy," she whispered. Noise assaulted her oversensitive ears. A symphony of a busy hospital played out. Food trays rattled down the hallway. Machines sent out cryptic messages in assorted beeps. Under it all droned muted voices of concern.

"So I'm not dead?"

A man chuckled, but her heart sank. It wasn't Dylan.

"You're not dead," the person with the light assured her as he clicked it off.

"But I wish I was," she grumbled, and closed her eyes. "How's Dylan Matthews?"

''Dylan is all right, honey,'' said her father, as his rough hand gripped hers on the bed railing. ''Someone else has come to see you. Evan Quade.''

''Where's Dylan?'' She hated the desperation in her voice, but she had to be sure he was all right.

''He's investigating the explosion, honey.''

''Explosion?'' What an incredible story! Her fingers itched to get the details down on paper.

''Yeah, the one that knocked you into his truck. You've gotta let this go, Lindsey. You have to see how dangerous it is. What's more important is that now he's seen it, too.''

She winced over the condemnation in her father's voice. ''That's why he's not here, Dad. He's protecting me again.''

''And doing a piss-poor job of it.'' Evan Quade threw in his unsolicited two cents.

Lindsey pried open an eyelid to glare at him. ''What are you doing here?''

''You're here.''

''You don't even know me.'' She narrowed her eyes on his handsome face.

''I heard about the explosion on the radio. Stopping here was on my way home. You're in Traverse City. They flew you here by emergency 'copter.''

''For a bump on the head?'' She snorted and ran shaking fingers over the bandage on her forehead. Beneath the gauze, the raised flesh throbbed.

Her father squeezed her free hand. ''A bump on the head can be serious, you know, honey. They had to check for swelling on the brain.''

''At last, everyone will know what a big brain I have.'' She teased a smile out of her father.

He shook his head, but his smile stayed.

Quade cleared his throat. "When I heard about the explosion and the injuries, I came to the hospital."

"To check your investment? I assume the mayor's dead?" The grim faces of both men confirmed her suspicion. "The mayor and Oliver are both out of the way. The rezone's a done deal now, the mall as good as built."

Quade's dark eyes didn't blink. "The sheriff will be a rich man now."

And if this man's suspicions were correct, Dylan would be crushed that his childhood hero was a killer. She had to go to him.

She glanced around, even though the room spun crazily at her sharp movement. The white-coated doctor was gone.

"Dad, find the doc, and spring me from this place, okay? There's too much going on. We can't be away from Winter Falls now."

Her father shook his head. "You need to stay here."

"If you don't spring me, I'll walk out with my hospital gown flapping open behind me." She rose from the pillows, but the effort left her dizzy and queasy. She fought to hang on to consciousness.

"You're such a brat," he grumbled, and ran his hand over her messy hair. Then he walked out.

"You can leave," she told Quade.

He opened his mouth, but the ringing of the phone stopped whatever pronouncement he'd been about to make. As if he had every right, he reached for the phone on her bedside table.

"Hello. Yes, this is Quade." The dark-haired man smiled, and Lindsey's uneasiness increased.

She held out a hand for the phone.

"Deputy Dylan," he said as he passed it to her.

"You're okay?" was his first question.

Lindsey's heart softened. "Yes."

"What the hell is he doing there? You're not alone with him?"

His harsh tone stung. As always, she reacted to pain with sarcasm. "At least he's here with me."

Dylan growled. "Don't push me, Lindsey. I was thinking of your safety."

She laughed. "Protecting me again, Dylan? You think he's going to smother me with a pillow?"

"I can't believe the mayor's house blew up. You shouldn't have—" His voice broke with emotion. "I didn't   "

She melted into the pillows, her pain forgotten. "I know you didn't, Dylan. It wasn't your fault."

"That's not what your father thinks."

"I take it he came to the scene?"

"Yeah, but it doesn't matter. He's right. You don't belong in the middle of a dangerous police investigation."

"Thank you for telling me that. But I've been there before." And her ex-fiancé had had no problem with her handling the dangerous end of research. He'd taken the glory by putting his byline on a story he would not have had without her legwork.

"I wasn't with you in Chicago. But I am with you now. You're not going to get hurt because of me!"

Before she could respond to that, the connection broke. He'd hung up on her.

"Damn him," she muttered, and slammed the receiver down with the little strength she had left.

"The lawman laying down the law?" Quade quipped.

"Cute." She closed her eyes and ran her fingers over the gauze again. "I thought you were leaving." It wasn't a question.

He shrugged. "I might wait to see what the doctor has to say about your injuries."

"Why?" Her eyes snapped opened, and exasperation had her sputtering. "I don't get it. You don't even know me. Why are you here?"

"You're going through a rough time. I'm human. I care about people."

She laughed. "Pull the other one." Her mirth faded fast. "I need to be home. My mother's missing. Since you seem to know everything, you must know that."

"Yeah, I know that." A hard edge brought bitterness to his response. He turned to the window, presenting her with the back of his expertly tailored suit.

"So you know I need to get out of here!" In Lindsey's mind there was nothing more frustrating than helplessness. And she'd been frustrated most of her life.

"Why?"

"Why what?" she snapped, and fought to pull away from the pillows again. Her carnival ride picked up so much speed, she couldn't see the scenery. She subsided against the stiff pillows.

"Why do you act as if you care about your mother?"

"Act? What?"

"I mean, you and your dad put her in an insane asylum, and in all these years, how many times have you visited her?"

"What do you know about it? It's not any of your business! Just who the hell do you think you are?" Her shouting nearly shattered her head, but anger had her by the throat. And guilt flooded it all.

"Your brother."

"You're insane!"

He turned back to her then, and although he wavered in and out of her distorted vision, she realized how very serious he was.

THE HOUR WAS LATER than sensible for a jog, due to the dim light of dusk, but Dylan needed the slap of his running shoes against the pavement. He needed the rhythmic noise of the rubber soles against the asphalt. He needed the burn in his lungs and shins.

But still he couldn't outrun his demons. He'd handed her to Quade. While Dylan should have been at her bedside, holding her hand, promising to cherish her for the rest of his life, Quade was there instead. Moving in.

And Lindsey was moving on. She wouldn't stay in Winter Falls. She'd stated that, had been honest and up front.

He was the one who'd broken the rules. He, the lawman. He'd fallen in love with her. He'd probably always been in love with her, even when she'd been a feisty teenager. Perhaps that was why he'd never allowed himself a serious relationship.

He'd told himself he wasn't a good risk. His job was too dangerous. His past too painful. A woman didn't need a man like him in her life.

Lindsey didn't need him. She was better off without him.

He pounded the pavement into town. Sweat streaked from his hair and flowed into his eyes, burning them. He welcomed the pain.

Mindless of his sweat-stained clothes and rapid breaths, Dylan jumped onto the sidewalk and pulled open the door to the diner.

The dinner hour had long passed.

"Hey, Marge!"

When Marge glanced up from wiping down the counter, she glared. Dylan turned on his heel, the rubber sole squeaking against the vinyl tiled floor.

"That was cold, Dylan, accusing the man of murder. He loves you like a son."

He pinched the bridge of his nose. How had he forgotten how fast word got around in Winter Falls? "I was doing my job, Marge." Dylan forced away the guilt and the suspicion, made it impersonal. He remembered his duty. "I have to find who committed these murders. I—"

She nodded and patted a hand over her blond hair. "I know, Dylan. But it's nasty. Are you going to arrest him?"

"I can't say, Marge." He sighed. "I'll never get over how quickly rumors spread in this town. And nobody forgets, no matter how much time passes."

She sniffed. "The rumors keep the dead alive."

Into his mind sprang an image of a laughing Jimmy. Maybe that was why he'd come home, more than his personal vow to clear his name.

He blew out a ragged breath. "Maybe the past should be kept there, Marge. It's pointless to talk about it."

"Sometimes the past comes back to haunt us, Dylan. Sometimes it can't just lie." Marge's smile didn't brighten the sadness in her eyes.

He'd never dealt with his feelings regarding Jimmy's death, or his parents', for that matter. Maybe he should plan on taking Mrs. Warner's vacated bed at Arborview.

"You want something? A bottle of water?"

Dylan shook his head. "No, I have to get back to my jog."

"Where you headed? The sheriff just left. He wouldn't talk about it, either. Just said you moved out."

He ran a hand through his sweat-dampened hair. For a lot of reasons he couldn't talk about the sheriff. "Maybe I'll swing by the Warners', check on the officer who's watching for Mrs. Warner's return."

"Check on Lindsey," she said with a smile.

Dylan shook his head. "The hospital would have kept her for observation."

Marge arched a brow. "That headstrong girl?"

"Who? Lindsey Warner?" he said, with a feeble attempt to lift his lips into a smile.

Marge politely chuckled as he pulled open the door to jog off into the gathering dusk.

Chapter Eleven

Dylan stopped at the crossroads. One path led to the sheriff's house, the other to Lindsey. Was Marge right? Was Lindsey home? Was she resting? Or hurting?

His heart ached, and not from physical exertion. He longed to see her impish face. His arms tingled with the desire to wrap around her small, curvy body and just hold her. Hold her close. As he had after the explosion. The paramedics had had to literally pull him away until he'd come to his senses.

Until he'd shut it off. He needed to do that now. He needed to ignore his aching heart and bypass the road to Lindsey. Every time he came close to her, he put her in danger. Each incident had become more perilous.

Just by being, he was a threat to her safety. He blinked away the sweat burning his eyes and he shivered as the night air penetrated his damp clothes. He had to head home, wherever that was.

His muscles ached, but he forced himself into motion. He jogged toward the sheriff's house. He wouldn't talk to him, not yet. He'd just check that the old man's car was parked in the drive. Then he'd head back to the impersonal motel room he'd rented.

Around him, the breeze rustled through the remaining leaves on the trees. The fallen ones crunched beneath his feet as he ran.

The shrillness of a car horn shattered the quiet of the autumn evening. Dylan glanced behind him, around him, but the noise came from a distance yet. Ahead. Toward the sheriff's. He pushed himself, forcing his weary muscles to greater speed.

A half of a mile ahead, he glimpsed the sheriff's old police cruiser. The front end had slammed into an enormous oak at the edge of a curve in the back country road.

Dylan scrambled around the car and tried to wrench open the driver's door. The twisted metal refused to budge. Through the shattered glass of the driver's window, he saw the portly sheriff pinned between the steering wheel and his seat, leaning on the horn. The old man's eyes were closed.

"Damn it!" He slammed his fist into the glass, knocking shards to the ground. A few stray pieces penetrated the flesh of his forearm. A bite of pain drew a curse from him. He shut it off.

He checked the sheriff's wide neck, searching desperately for a pulse. No beat was discernible beneath the thick flesh.

Automatically he reached for the car radio and sent up brief thanks that it wasn't crushed. He forced his voice to steady as he called for help.

With trembling fingers he searched for the lever beside the seat and forced it back. Carefully he loos-

ened the sheriff's seat belt and eased him to his side.
Then he began chest compressions.

Even though he shoved back the emotions, his
thoughts taunted him. Had his interrogation of the
sheriff brought on a heart attack? What other reason
would have caused the sheriff to run off a road he
had traveled so often?

Old pain rolled over the new. He closed his eyes
and for the second time that day he fervently prayed.
And he hoped his prayers would be answered again.

"I DON'T KNOW IF IT'S a good idea to tell the deputy."
Evan Quade maneuvered around a sharp turn.

Lindsey grasped his arm when he reached for the
clutch in his cramped sports car. "Stop. There's a
wreck!" She peered through the darkness at the car
crumpled against a tree.

A tall, lean man loomed beside the car. Even from
a distance, Lindsey sensed his desperation in the agitated motion of his hands. The headlights glinted off
his golden hair. Panic clawed through her. Dylan.

"Stop!" she yelled again.

"Okay." Quade screeched the car to a halt.

She vaulted out before he turned off the ignition.
"Dylan! What happened? Are you all right?" She
grabbed his arm to pull him toward her. Blood oozed
between her fingers. "You're hurt!"

"I wasn't in the accident. I'm fine. It's Sheriff
Buck." Dylan jerked a hand toward the car.

"How bad is he hurt?" Quade asked, his cell
phone cradled in his hand.

"I already called it in. Thank God the radio was

working." Dylan jerked his bloody arm from Lindsey's fingers and ran his hand through his tousled hair.

"I'm okay, boy!" the sheriff gasped in a poor imitation of his notorious bellow.

"You're not okay." Dylan's words escaped through his clenched teeth.

"What the hell do you think? I wake up to you giving me mouth to mouth." The old man spat onto the gravel shoulder of the road as he twisted in the shortened front seat of the car. He could probably free himself despite the closeness of the steering wheel, but Dylan's imposing stance prevented him from trying.

"Thank God you're all right," Lindsey said, and reached down to squeeze the old man's shoulder.

"Thank the boy." The sheriff's voice broke, and he rubbed a knuckle into his tearing eye. "Fool kid jogging all around the countryside. Lucky for me, though."

Lindsey blinked back tears at the sight of the sheriff's affection for Dylan.

"Yeah," Dylan rasped, "lucky for you. I know how this happened. It was my fault."

"A lot of stuff seems to be your fault," Quade commented, and Lindsey shot him an annoyed grimace.

"And you keep turning up." Dylan's sharp gaze swung toward Quade.

Her brother shrugged.

Lindsey reached for Dylan's arm again. "You're hurt." She gingerly touched a fingertip to the glass embedded in his skin. "This is really nasty. We have to stop the bleeding."

"I'm fine." Dylan tried to pull free again, but she tightened her hold on him.

Due to the cool night air and her insistent father, she'd worn a sweater. She shrugged out of it, dropping his arm only long enough to free hers. She caught his hand again and loosely wrapped the cashmere around his bleeding forearm.

"Lindsey," he protested. "You're ruining your sweater. Come on…"

"It's just a sweater," she said dismissively. But it had cost a day's salary.

"Why are you here?" He stared down at her makeshift bandage.

"We have something to tell you. It can wait now."

Dylan caught her chin in his hand and glided his fingertips over her cheekbone to the bandage on her forehead. "You're all right? You shouldn't be out of the hospital." His gaze slid to Quade. "And you shouldn't be with him. There're things you don't know, Lindsey. I checked him out."

She nodded, tears over his concern stinging her eyes. "I—I have things to tell you, too."

Distant sirens heralded the ambulance. He sighed. "It'll have to wait." The ambulance approached, its lights flashing. He caught the lapel of Quade's jacket in his bloodied fist. "If anything happens to her…"

Quade nodded. "She's safe. Safer with me than you." His dark eyes gleamed.

Dylan shoved the other man back and strode to the sheriff's crumpled car.

Lindsey reached for the passenger door of the sports car. "Let's get out of the way."

Quade ran his fingers over the wrinkled lapel. "Yes, now is not the time to talk to him about this."

Lindsey shook her head and ignored the hustle of paramedics as they rushed to the sheriff. "You didn't want to tell him, anyway. But not now. He's upset."

"Despite threatening me, he doesn't seem that concerned about you. Never came to see you. Although he had no way of knowing you were out of the hospital, he was out jogging tonight."

Lindsey glanced back at the wreck. The sheriff waved away the paramedics and stood up with Dylan's help, his pudgy arm wrapped around his young friend's shoulders. She remembered the sheriff's words about Dylan trying to outrun his pain.

"Actually, his running is a sign in my favor. But I'm not interested."

"Oh, you're not?" Quade's lips twisted into a mocking smile.

She watched Dylan help the paramedics lift the sheriff's stretcher into the back of the ambulance. Then he hopped into it, too. He never looked back at her before the doors closed. Lindsey blinked back the threat of tears.

Quade slid behind the wheel, and she marveled that such a tall man would choose to drive such a tiny car. "You're making the fatal mistake."

"What's that? You can't believe Sarah Hutchins's paranoid ranting about Dylan!" Disappointment washed over her, and she shivered in the chill night air. A few snowflakes danced in the darkness and kissed the windshield. She shivered again.

Quade turned on the heater. The blast of warm air didn't dissipate the chill.

"I'd say it is funny that all this stuff happened the minute he strolled back into town."

"He wasn't the only one to come back now. I did, too. And I don't believe you or the Hutchinses have been here long. Just long enough to stir up trouble, proposing a controversial project."

"I kinda like stirring up trouble."

She had to laugh. "So that is genetic." She allowed a dry chuckle to escape.

Quade executed a sharp turn to head them back toward Lindsey's home. "I would keep your eyes open. Sometimes people you think you know do unexpected things."

"Dylan is not responsible for any of this," Lindsey insisted. "There's no way." But she wondered if his return hadn't set into motion the tragedies that had struck Winter Falls.

Quade shrugged. "You're doing it."

"What?" God, the man was annoying. So this was what it was like to have a brother? And she resented all the years she'd missed.

"You're trying too hard. You're giving up everything you have and are to make this person happy, to make this person want to 'keep' you. I thought that feeling was exclusive to adopted children."

Lindsey squeezed her eyes shut against a wave of pain for them both. "You've done that?"

His nod was short, and she glimpsed the tension in his jaw despite the dim light.

"I've done that, too," she admitted. "You thought she gave you up? That she didn't want you?"

"That's usually how adopted children feel, that their birth parents didn't want them. That they weren't good enough to keep."

Lindsey laid her hand over his on the leather-wrapped steering wheel. "She wanted you. She never wanted to give you up. I don't think she ever did in her heart."

He turned his hand over and squeezed hers back. She thought it a rare show of affection for him. "Thanks."

"She loves you."

"I know that now. But it still feels too late...."

Lindsey couldn't argue with that. She stared through the windshield at the sparsely falling snowflakes. "At the hospital you showed me your birth certificate, but you never told me how you got it. Are you the one who broke into Chet Oliver's office?"

He chuckled. "Breaking and entering? You do believe the rumors about me."

"I don't know the rumors about you."

"Your deputy does." He sighed. "But know this, they're just rumors. I hired a private investigator to find my birth parents. He brought me a box of records he bribed off a guard at Arborview."

"So that's how you got them."

He nodded. "The private investigator traced my birth to the home and got the records. I don't know why he gave me all of them. The information is incomplete, regardless—my father unknown.''

She could admire his tenacity, if not his methods. But she worried that the rest of the information he sought was locked in the mind of a woman who may never be lucid enough to release it. ''Can you drop me at the hospital?''

''I'd like to think you want to go there because you regret checking yourself out against the doctor's wishes. But that's not it.''

''No.''

''Did you listen to anything I said?''

Unfortunately she had. ''I'm trying too hard, so what! But this isn't about Dylan and me anymore. After all that's happened, I'm not a big believer in accidents. I need to know what happened here. The public needs to know.''

''I'm sure Deputy Dylan is checking into it.''

''You know what this means?''

''That you have no reason to go to the hospital.''

''What it means is there's a serial killer in Winter Falls. Two men have died. Maybe the sheriff was supposed to be number three.''

''I doubt it, Lindsey. This looks more like the work of a person with a score to settle. Something he came home after a decade to do.''

She tensed. ''You're wrong. Drop me at the hospital.''

''And then what?''

''You're right. Drop me home. I'll borrow Dad's car.''

"You were told not to drive yet. You have a knock on your head, remember?"

Since it throbbed incessantly, she could hardly forget. But she needed to see Dylan. Two attempts had been made on his life. No doubt existed in her mind that the killer intended Deputy Dylan Matthews to be the next victim.

DYLAN STOPPED AT THE FOOT of the hospital bed to glance at the sheriff one more time. Despite the monitors beeping around him, the old man slept peacefully, snoring as loudly as he spoke. Dylan smiled and opened the door.

He nodded to the Traverse City police officer he'd requested posted to guard the sheriff.

Then his gaze shot beyond him to Lindsey Warner. She had curled up in a vinyl chair in the hallway, her head resting on one knee. Her dark lashes lay against the bluish shadows below her eyes. He could have walked right past her. She would not realize he was gone until she awoke.

With a sharp pang, his heart protested the thought. He knelt beside her and brushed a knuckle across the satiny softness of her cheek.

Her long lashes fluttered apart. In that unguarded moment her dark eyes brimmed with an emotion that caused Dylan's heart to leap and then clutch with fear.

"Hi," she murmured with a sleepy smile.

"Hi yourself," he said, and he tried to harden his heart. He tried to think of her safety, and that just being around him threatened it. "What are you doing here?"

"I came to talk to you."

He remembered her words at the crash site. She had something to tell him. She'd been with Evan Quade. He rose to his feet. "It's going to have to wait. I'm really busy right now."

"How are you getting home?" She stood behind him now. Her arm brushed his.

He stopped at the automatic exit doors to the hospital. "Well…"

"You're not going to get a taxi to take you to Winter Falls tonight."

"I'm not?" He tightened his jaw over the acknowledgment that she was right.

"No, but you can get a ride home with me."

"You drove? You took a knock on the head. Should you be driving?" He turned back to scan her weary face.

Under a fall of curls, a small bandage covered a bruised area on her forehead. When he squeezed his eyes closed, he could see the explosion propel her toward his Expedition.

"I could, but Dad dropped me and the car off and Evan picked him up." She slid past him and through the automatic doors.

He caught her in the parking lot beside a white Pontiac. "Your mother's stolen car?"

She nodded. "That's part of what I have to tell you. You're the acting sheriff now that the sheriff's hurt? I tried to get past the guard at his door, but he said no one was allowed in but you. What's going on, Dylan? Was this another attack?"

"Always the reporter, Lindsey? You're about to fall on your face but you still fire questions at me."

"Are we just a reporter and a lawman, Dylan?"

He closed his eyes again and debated his ability to drive the dark roads to Winter Falls. He already knew there was no way Lindsey was getting behind the wheel. After a mental shake, he held out his hand for the keys to the car.

With a sigh she dropped them in his palm. "You're all chauvinists."

"No, we're too smart to ride with you. You were dangerous enough before your brains were scrambled." He held the passenger's door for her and steadied her as she stumbled a bit while sliding into her seat. "Are you all right?"

She nodded and slumped back. He pulled the seat belt around her, sliding the strap over her shoulder, over the enticing curve of her breast under her black turtleneck sweater, and snapped it into the clasp at her hip. Her quick, shallow breaths whispered against his cheek. "Dylan..."

He jerked back, ignoring the flash of pain from the metal of the car roof connecting with the back of his head. He slammed the door and stalked around to the driver's side. Before he could find the ignition, she skimmed her fingers lightly over the bandage on his forearm.

"Someone saw to your arm." The harsh parking lot lights illuminated the interior of the car, heightening the white of his bandage and the paleness of her face. A faint smile twisted her lips.

"Your sweater—"

"It doesn't matter."

"I think it's with the sheriff's things." He'd made them keep it. "I'm sure it's ruined. I'll buy you another."

"Doesn't matter. It was just a sweater."

"I'll reimburse you."

"And they say I'm stubborn. Okay, reimburse me. It was a hundred dollars."

"For a sweater?"

"Why are we discussing a sweater?"

He maneuvered the car onto the street and pointed it in the direction of Winter Falls, although he'd rather have gone anywhere else. "Because I need conversation to keep me awake. What did you have to tell me? How'd you get the car back?"

"First, why the guard?"

"I can't trust anyone."

"Even me?" Her voice broke with pain and indignation. The indignation he could handle.

"Even you. You're keeping strange company nowadays. I checked out Hutchins and Quade right after Chet's murder."

"And?"

"Off the record for now?"

"That was our deal, but can you really trust me?"

"That's what I'd like to know." He sighed. "Hutchins always gets what he goes after. He's incredibly rich and powerful. Sarah's father worked for him in Chicago, which is where they moved after—" he forced himself to go on "—after Jimmy and Steve died."

"And Quade?"

"I don't trust him. I guess Hutchins is like every extremely wealthy businessman who likes to have his own guard dog, his own protection..."

"I thought Quade was his real estate adviser."

"That, too," Dylan conceded.

"And?"

"And his hired gun."

"Quade doesn't carry a gun." She snorted.

Dylan shrugged. "He has a dangerous background. Some people believe he murdered his wife. Nobody would hire him because of that, except Hutchins. He must feel an awesome loyalty to this man, perhaps enough to do whatever Hutchins requested."

"Even kill?" Her tone was too mild for him to believe he'd gotten through to her. "But he was acquitted of his wife's murder?"

"He was never brought to trial. A body was never found. But an investigation was done. Friends of mine in the Chicago department believe he's just too smart to be caught."

He thought of Lindsey alone with him, in danger. He fought down the panic. Then he glanced in the rearview mirror and was reassured by the headlight beams behind him. As he'd ordered after the explosion, Deputy Jones was sticking close to Lindsey.

"He lived in Chicago all those years I lived there." She sighed.

Dylan's heart clutched with fear again. "And you regret that you never met? You move fast, Lindsey. You've made up for lost time. Can't you understand why you should stay away from him? He's a dangerous man!'' He tore his eyes from the road to glance at her pale face, luminescent in the dim lights of the dashboard.

"He's my brother."

Chapter Twelve

"What?" Dylan managed to say after a few moments of silence. He didn't know if he dared to continue this bizarre conversation while he drove the dark roads. But he had to know.

"Yes, Evan Quade is my brother. All these years, in her madness, my mother sought her son, and all these years, he sought her. But Evan's not mad. He's methodical."

"I still think he's dangerous. And I want to say I don't care who he is, but I can't."

"It matters to you that he's my brother?" Her fingers brushed over his bandaged arm.

Hope swelled in her voice, the echo of her youthful crush from all those years ago. He wanted to quash it, but for selfish reasons he couldn't. "I don't know, Lindsey. How can you believe he's not involved?"

"Not in the deaths of Chet and the mayor. No, but he's involved in other things...."

Dylan's shock had his fingers tightening on the steering wheel. "You knew about his wife?"

In the reflection in the windshield, Dylan caught her waving a hand in dismissal. "Not like you're thinking. She ran off. Her murder was just a rumor. No proof existed. It never even came to trial. You just admitted that.''

"Yeah." His admission accompanied a heavy sigh. Rumor had made him a killer, too. "So what did he do?"

"He found my mother."

"What?" He worried that the conversation should have waited until the car was parked. He didn't need to be involved in another accident. He thought of pulling off the road, but they were only minutes from his motel room. "You mean he kidnapped her?"

"No, but he had an inside connection at Arborview. This guy called him, warned him she was out again. He got to my house first. She was sitting in her car in the driveway."

"And he didn't take her back to the sanatorium? He didn't notify the police or you?" Anger surged through him. How could the man who claimed to be her brother have put Lindsey through such anguish?

"Well, he thought she was in danger. She didn't get out on her own. Someone was framing her as someone framed him a few years ago. He wanted to protect her."

"Nice guy," Dylan sneered. "So does he know who's been getting her out?"

Her ragged sigh stirred the air near his arm. "No. He had to take her to a private psychiatric hospital. She's pretty messed up."

Alarm shot through him. "Hurt?"

"No. She's uncommunicative."

"So Quade couldn't possibly have shot at us because he was busy kidnapping your mother."

"He did not kidnap her. He found her. And she went with him willingly."

"She's cr—" He caught himself, but the damage was done. No comeback emanated from Lindsey but a hurt-filled silence. "I'm sorry," he said, and meant it.

"Normally I'd agree with you. She's crazy. She's been crazy for years, but Quade doesn't think so. He thinks that Arborview kept her overmedicated. He thinks he can help her. He has her under the care of a highly respected private psychiatrist."

"And you trust him with your mother's care? You believe he's who he says he is?" Conversely Dylan wanted to protect and shatter her innocence.

"Hell, no, not on his word alone. I checked it out. He has the missing records from Arborview. He has his original birth certificate."

"And he shows all this to you after you've been knocked out by an explosion. He gets you at your most vulnerable, and you believe him. He broke into Chet's office."

"No, he didn't. He bribed a guard—"

Dylan struck the steering wheel. "The conveniently vanished guard. The one person who could corroborate any of his story. I can't believe you're buying this."

"I'm not a fool, not anymore. I don't believe in heroes, in the goodness of man. I don't think it's there. I think you accept what you get, and you grow up. I grew up a while ago, Dylan."

He chuckled. "You're not the tough, cynical reporter you pretend to be, Lindsey. You're a marshmallow inside, and you're going to get hurt."

"Again? Probably. But it's better to risk that than to lock up all my emotions and never experience anything life has to offer. Not the happiness. Not the pain. If I'm a fool, oh, well. But you're a coward, Dylan Matthews. And I'd rather be a fool any day."

Dylan clenched his jaw and spoke succinctly. "You ever figure that maybe the happiness isn't worth the pain?"

Lindsey sighed. "I'd like to argue with you, but then I don't know."

"You've never been happy?" He thought of the diamond ring she'd carried in her bag.

"I don't know. Have you ever been happy, Dylan? I guess you already answered that question."

"I guess I have." He turned the car toward the section of town where new motels had been constructed.

"I should take you home," he said. "You've been through a lot today, yesterday, probably tomorrow. It's not safe for you to be around me. And it seems like this killer never sleeps. But I don't want to take you home, Lindsey."

"You want to talk some more?" A teasing lilt accompanied her question.

He groaned. "I'm tired of talking, and I'm tired of thinking."

She laughed. "Then what does that leave for us to do, Dylan?"

He laughed, too. She never failed to amaze him.

Even with all she'd been through in the last week, she kept her humor and her spunk and her determination.

Perhaps simply being around her would inspire him to find those qualities within himself. Yet, the pure selfishness of risking her safety for his own purposes told him he'd never be half the person she was. And eventually she'd leave him, as everyone else had.

He pulled the Bonneville into the lot beside his black Expedition. Few other vehicles occupied the lot and only a couple of lights burned in the nearby rooms.

"I wonder," he mused aloud, "if any of this would have happened if I hadn't come back."

"What are you saying?" Lindsey's fingers played lightly over his arm again.

"It's me."

She clenched her fingers, but he welcomed the sting of pain.

"You're not—"

"Oh, God, no!" he exclaimed, and his heart hurt that even for a moment she could believe him capable of murder. "You thought—"

"No! Absolutely not!"

He twisted his mouth but doubted it resembled a smile. "What's that about protesting too much?"

"I'm not. I don't think you're involved. I never did," she insisted.

"But others do. This town has always thought the worst of me. I should be used to it."

"But you're not." Her fingers slid from his arm. "I'm sorry. I didn't mean—"

"I know." He caught her hand and brought it to his mouth to brush a kiss across her knuckles. "It's okay."

"No, it's not."

"I meant that I'm the catalyst. I'm the reason this all started. I'm the reason you're in danger. And the sheriff. And the mayor and Chet are dead."

"So the mayor was inside the house?"

"It was confirmed tonight. A candle burning in the kitchen and a gas leak from the stove."

"You're not suggesting it's an accident."

He shook his head. "No. No town can have this many accidents. But someone's very clever and very dangerous."

He slid the key back in the ignition. "I really should take you home."

She clasped her hand over his and pulled out the key. "No, you shouldn't. Let's go inside, Dylan."

As they'd driven up, he'd surreptitiously scanned the area. He couldn't see anyone lying in wait for them. Jones's car pulled to the curb on the side street. But he was careful as he stepped around the car and opened her door. Then he kept her sheltered between his body and the white stucco motel.

"I know what you're doing." She leaned into him and chuckled.

"You're not supposed to know. It makes you mad."

"When you're protecting me? I'm getting used to it, and that's the sad part."

"Because you'll be leaving soon…"

She turned her head and gazed up at him. But his

shadow obscured her eyes. He couldn't read whatever emotion lurked there.

"That's for the best." He tried to convince himself. "This town was never what you wanted."

"No, the town never was..." She laid her hand over his. "You already rented a room?"

"I'm not staying at the sheriff's anymore." He wouldn't be welcome. He'd packed before he'd searched his old friend's house.

"The taxidermy get to you? Or did you talk to the sheriff about owning the land?"

He blew out a ragged breath. "There are things I should tell you...."

He slid the key into the door lock and pushed it open. He guided her just across the threshold, and closed and locked the door behind her. Then he strode into the bathroom for a quick check.

"All clear?" She lifted a brow.

He nodded. "It's not funny."

"I know." She sighed. "It's just that this is Winter Falls. It's not Detroit or Chicago. It's supposed to be safe, secure. You shouldn't have to lock your doors."

"And we were safer in those big cities than we are in our own hometown," Dylan concurred. "Yeah, sad."

"It's not your fault," she said. "Whoever is behind this would have committed these crimes even if you hadn't come home."

Dylan shrugged off the hope her words inspired. "I'd like to believe that, but I can't."

"You don't even know who—" She narrowed her dark eyes. "You do."

Dylan shook his head. "No, there're too many suspects."

"Tell me who they are. I can help you narrow it down."

"I don't think so." He longed to confide in her, to pour out all his suspicions and listen to the quick work of her clever mind. But to do so would put her in danger. He couldn't bear to see her hurt again.

"What are you up to?"

"Police work," he said. "I have to get evidence." He hoped he lived up to the citations he'd been awarded—the ones that the sheriff had kept in a scrapbook on top of murder evidence. "I have to figure this out before someone else gets hurt."

Lindsey smiled. "And you won't give a scoop to a reporter."

Dylan crossed the remaining feet separating them. "I'll tell you when I'm sure."

He slid a hand into her hair, brushing the tangle of curls from the bandage on her forehead. He dropped a light kiss against the gauze. "Do you want to leave?" He caught her chin in his hand and tipped her face up to his. Circles as dark as her eyes bruised the skin beneath them. Exhaustion.

She shook her head, wobbling her chin in his grip. "No! I want to stay, Dylan. I want you."

"You're exhausted, concussed."

"But I still want you. I guess some things never change." She rose on tiptoe and pressed her mouth to his.

Dylan struggled with the pleasure coursing through

his body. His pulse leaped. His heart raced. He wanted her. But more than that, he needed her.

One kiss followed another, lips locking, tongues sliding over each other. Unable to shut away his feelings, his desires, he lifted and carried her to the bed.

"Lindsey." He followed her down on the hard mattress. "I—"

She silenced him with her fingers across his lips. "No talking. Remember? You're tired of talking, and you're tired of thinking. Just feel." She wriggled out from underneath him enough to pull her shirt over her head. Her dark curls danced around her naked shoulders. Sinuously she slid her pants down over her hips, leaving her clad only in the briefest pieces of silk and lace.

"Lindsey..." She'd been hurt. He didn't want to hurt her more.

Her mouth silenced him next. He pressed her into the mattress, as he took the kiss deeper. She pushed against his chest.

"Lindsey?"

"Too many clothes." She tsked, then yanked his shirt over his head and dragged his sweats over his hips.

"I forgot." He pulled away. "My run. I need to take a shower."

"Later." Her lips ran across his chest, targeted a nipple and made him shudder with his desire for her. "We'll take one together. I like to watch you in the shower."

"Lindsey, you're going to rush it."

"Rush it. Rush it," she urged. She snagged his

navy briefs next, pushing them down with the glide of her nails over his skin.

He needed to taste her, really taste her. He started at her throat, running the tip of his tongue over her jumping pulse. With his teeth he dragged down the strap of her bra from one shoulder until her freed breast thrust toward him. Then he lapped at it, circling the erect nipple until she slid her fingers into his hair and pulled him closer. He took the straining tip in his mouth, and she moaned.

"Dylan." A ragged breath sighed out of her parted lips. "Please, rush it."

"No rushing." And he took his time. He tasted every inch of her until she tore the sheets from the mattress, writhing beneath his lips.

From the shaving kit he'd tossed next to the bed, he pulled out a condom and donned protection.

Then he rushed it. But her keening cry of pleasure told him he didn't go alone into ecstasy. He stroked the tangled curls back from her face and pressed another light kiss to the gauze on her forehead.

He wanted to give her words he'd never given another. He wanted to express feelings he'd never felt. And it hadn't been because he hadn't allowed himself, but because there had never been anyone like Lindsey.

He opened his mouth but rethought the wisdom of giving her the words. He had nothing else to offer her. No home. A shaky career. Would she wait around while he rebuilt his life? He doubted it. She'd found her mother and her brother. Once the killer was caught, she'd leave again.

He tucked her close to his side and hung on tightly as he slipped into a light sleep. He had to listen for any peculiar noise. He had to keep her safe. Even from himself.

LINDSEY AWOKE WITH A DRY mouth and a throbbing headache. But she was alive, never more alive, and never more in love. Her foolish heart had made another mistake. But it didn't matter. She'd never felt so much before. Even though her love was not returned, she couldn't stop loving him.

Discovering her arms empty, she opened her eyes and glanced around the impersonal motel room. On the nightstand his wallet lay open.

Next to his badge was a picture of a golden-haired, blue-eyed angel. His mother. And Dylan had watched her die. She shuddered for the loss of his childhood and longed to soothe away his pain.

Then she spotted him beside the window. He'd tipped open the blinds to peer out. She wondered if he watched the sunrise and appreciated its glorious pinks and purples streaking across a slate sky. Or did he watch for enemies and danger and miss the beauty entirely? She worried that he did the latter, had done so his whole life.

Yet, how much beauty had he known in his life? A man who didn't think happiness was worth the pain? A man who thought one couldn't be obtained without the other.

"Hypocrite," she accused herself in a harsh whisper. What did she know about happiness or beauty?

"What?" Dylan asked, but he didn't turn around.

Her gaze slid over the smooth muscles in his naked back, and she wanted him again. Who was she fooling? She wanted him always.

"Talking to myself," she muttered, and brushed a hand through the rat's nest that was her hair.

"How's the head?"

"Throbbing. I feel like I'm coming down from a three-day drinking binge, but without any embarrassing memories of it. Just the pain."

"I can find you something...."

She waved a hand at him as a yawn claimed her. A few hours of sleep would never suffice again. When this whole mess was over, she planned on sleeping ten hours every night. At least for a week.

"You want to go somewhere for breakfast?"

"No. I want answers."

"You're not going to like them." He sighed and ran a hand through his tousled hair. "I have to interview your mother, Lindsey."

"My mother?" She'd thought he'd dropped her mother as a suspect. She figured he had focused on the sheriff even though she hoped Dylan would be spared the pain of arresting a man he cared about, whom he idolized.

"She seems to be in the middle of all of this, Lindsey."

She shook her head. "No. She's being framed, Dylan."

"Another reason to talk to her, to figure out how she got out the night of Oliver's murder."

She sighed. "She can't help you, Dylan. She can

barely speak. I thought you were looking at the sheriff.''

''I talked to him.'' He shrugged. ''I searched his house. I don't have enough—''

''But the money he's going to get from the land…'' Lindsey shivered. ''It can make people do crazy things—that much money.''

''The money's not for him.''

''Then…'' She glimpsed the pain and remorse on his face. Dylan wasn't as able to detach himself as he once had. ''For you. He's doing it for you.''

''And I just about accused him of murder.''

''So it's not the sheriff.'' She mentally checked him off her list.

''I can't say that, either.'' He pinched the bridge of his nose. ''And I need to talk to your brother, officially.''

She sputtered out a laugh and reached for her clothes. This was not a discussion to have when naked. ''You're crazy! Evan had nothing to do with the deaths of the mayor and Chet Oliver. I thought you believed that.''

''I do.''

She dragged her sweater over her head and clipped her bra beneath it. ''Then why—''

''I want the records he has from Arborview. And I need your mother's car for evidence.'' He exhaled a ragged breath. ''And I think Evan Quade knows more than he's saying.''

''That's nonsense.'' She pulled her pants over her hips and struggled with the snap with trembling fingers.

"That's breaking the law if he's withholding information pertinent to a police investigation."

"You don't like him?"

"No."

"I thought it was because you were jealous, that you cared about me." Her heart ached, and she rubbed her knuckles over it. "But that's not the case. You know he's my brother, and you still dislike him."

"He thinks he's above the law, Lindsey. No one's above the law."

"And that's all you are, isn't it, Dylan? Just a lawman. Not a friend. Not a lover."

"Lindsey..."

She stepped into her shoes. "Those are *Evan's* records."

"Yeah, he bought them. He may know more about the guard. And he should have immediately informed the police when he found your mother. At the very least, he should have told your father."

She glared at him. "My father understands and accepts what Evan did."

Dylan shrugged. "I don't. He has to explain it to me along with some other things."

"Why waste your time with Evan when you have a killer to arrest? Who is it, Dylan?"

He shook his head and ran a hand over his bare chest. "I can't narrow it down. I have to have more proof, Lindsey. I don't want details from my investigation showing up on the front page of the *Gazette*."

Her palm itched to slap him. "You don't trust me.

Even after last night and the night before, you still don't trust me?''

He shook his head again. And didn't even call after her when she stormed out. Lindsey fought back the tears as she winced over the deafening noise of the door slamming behind her.

She stomped through the parking lot, past her mother's car. Evidence. Gulls sang a lonesome song as they scoured the asphalt for crumbs.

Her brother was right. She tried too hard. But she hadn't reached Dylan. She finally began to accept that she never would.

But there was one person who could reach him yet. One person who could teach Dylan how to unlock the door holding all his emotions in....

Chapter Thirteen

Lindsey watched the approach of Sarah Hutchins as a reflection in the window she faced.

"Why'd you ask me here?" The woman stood in front of Evan's desk and spoke to the back of his chair.

With the toe of her hiking boot, Lindsey spun the high-back leather chair around to face the desk. "For me."

Sarah took a quick step back. "I have nothing to say to you." Her gaze darted from Lindsey to the window behind her.

"Nothing to me? That's probably true. You owe Dylan an explanation."

Sarah laughed. "What makes you think I owe Dylan Matthews anything?"

"He's not the father of your son. He's not the man who took advantage of your youthful crush, Sarah. That man's dead."

"And everybody thinks my brother killed him." Tears glimmered in Sarah's eyes. "That's not true."

"Then who did, Sarah?" Lindsey vaulted to her feet and leaned over the wide desk. "Who?"

Sarah danced back a couple of steps. "You're saying—you think I did?"

"If not Steve, who had a motive besides you?"

"Evan brought me here to let you accuse me of murder?" Rage twisted Sarah's delicate features. "I'm going to tell my husband."

Lindsey shook her head, amazed by Sarah's immaturity. "And what's he going to do about it? Fire his right-hand man?"

Sarah's gray eyes were cold like the barrel of a gun. "My husband will do anything for me. Anything."

Lindsey shivered, but she didn't doubt Sarah. "You know there are just a couple of things the deaths of the mayor and Chet Oliver have in common."

Sarah shrugged.

"Not going to guess?"

"This is ridiculous. But you always were into ridiculous games. Chasing Dylan Matthews like you did."

"Ten years ago."

"Oh, not now?" Sarah's brow lifted into a perfect arch.

Lindsey wanted to say she'd caught him now, but she couldn't utter the lie. "No, ten years ago, the mayor was the judge who sentenced your brother to life in prison, and Chet was his lawyer. The man who advised him to plead guilty. And the sheriff—"

"He's dead, too?"

Lindsey hoped she glimpsed surprise and not triumph in the other woman's eyes. But she was too exhausted to trust her instincts. "No. But he had an accident. He's in the hospital."

"So you're saying what these men have in common is my brother's death on their hands? Then Dylan Matthews should be dead, too." Without the bitterness twisting her features, Sarah probably would have been quite lovely. Lindsey only saw the ugliness.

"There have been attempts. A few. Must be awfully frustrating for whoever's behind these murders. Of course, unsuspecting, old men are easy to kill. Dylan has suspects. He told me."

"And I'm one of them?" Sarah smirked. "Warning me? Isn't that dangerous, Lindsey? Wouldn't I flee town with my son?"

"If you are the killer, then I'm taking a risk. But I think you're too arrogant to run, Sarah. As you said, your husband would do anything for you. I believe he has, and he would."

"Now you're accusing my husband?" Sarah's interest shifted to her nails. She buffed the highly polished tips with her thumb. "You really are risking a lawsuit for defamation of character. Mine and my husband's."

Lindsey shrugged. "There will be a lawsuit. Dylan will sue you for visitation. You'd be much smarter to let their relationship form on your terms."

Sarah's gray eyes flashed. "My terms are that there is no relationship." She turned for the door.

Lindsey took a deep breath. "I didn't mean to threaten you, Sarah."

"Like someone with as few means as you could

ever threaten me," she scoffed from the door. Her hand was on the knob, but she didn't turn it.

Lindsey acknowledged that with a brief nod. "You're probably right about that. But what if that's all you're right about? What if Dylan had nothing to do with your brother's suicide? What if your brother really killed Jimmy? Then you've kept Dylan from the only family he has left for no reason. Then you've acted just as unjustly as your brother."

"You know nothing about having a brother. About how it was between us. We may not have been blood relatives, but we were raised together. We were raised with love."

"Then you always had more than Dylan. And you're keeping from him the one person who may be able to reach his heart. Are you that cruel, Sarah? You who were raised with so much love?" Lindsey swallowed her envy over Sarah's idyllic childhood.

Sarah leaned her forehead against the door. "I need proof, Lindsey. I need something to prove that Dylan is worthy of my son. And your word is not good enough. You've always loved Dylan Matthews."

Lindsey blinked her burning eyes. "Yeah, I've loved foolishly before, Sarah. Just as you did. I have my eyes wide open now. He's a good man."

Sarah opened the door. "I need proof," she maintained, and she walked out.

Lindsey had nothing to offer her. For although she claimed she hadn't fallen foolishly this time, she didn't know enough about Dylan Matthews to offer proof. What kind of man was he when he could make love to her one minute and in the next suspect her brother and mother of murder?

DYLAN GLANCED UP FROM his desk when a big box dropped on the cluttered surface. Whatever papers weren't crushed beneath the load fell to the scuffed floor. He narrowed his tired eyes at the person who leaned over the box.

"Quade."

"Deputy."

"I assume these are the missing files."

"Very sharp, Deputy. These are from Arborview, a gift to me." Amusement danced in Quade's dark eyes.

"A gift?" Dylan didn't feel like arguing with the man. He could still see the hurt look on Lindsey's face. The woman constantly interfered with his police work even when she wasn't present. "Without proof, I guess I'll have to accept that."

Quade laughed. "She got to you."

"I'm too busy to bother pinning a B and E charge on you," Dylan hedged, and dragged some papers from under the edge of the box.

Quade slid the box over, crumpling more papers, and perched on the corner of the desk. "She's gotten to me, too."

Dylan raised a brow.

"Not like that. She is my sister." Quade smiled. "And she's a very special lady. Smart, funny, loyal... A man could do worse."

"A man could do a lot worse. You matchmaking, Quade? I didn't figure you for the type."

He ran a hand over his dark hair. "No. You wouldn't be my first choice for Lindsey, probably not even my tenth."

Dylan couldn't argue with him, and he found himself softening a little over Quade's brotherly concern for Lindsey. "I trust all the files are here?"

"Everything that was left from when Arborview was the home for unwed mothers. First, I tried to bribe the truth out of the old man, but Chet thought sleeping dogs should lie." Quade snorted. "He was the dog. He never got my mother's signature, just her parents'. Bad deal all around."

"Other bad deals in there?"

"From what I could tell, yeah." Quade tapped a knuckle against the box.

"And everything was from years and years ago?" He didn't fully accept that these were the records from the home. He wouldn't put it past Quade to have broken into the old lawyer's office. If he had stolen those records, he may have taken other information from the lawyer. Like something from a man who died ten years ago...

"Yeah, the home closed up about twenty years ago. Everything in there is at least that old."

Dylan nodded but persisted. "Nothing more recent. Ten years old. I'm not talking about an adoption. Any correspondence, anything from ten years ago?"

Quade shook his head. "Not that I noticed, but I wouldn't have paid much attention to it. Obviously, I'm more than ten years old. So, you going to slap the cuffs on me for interfering with your investigation?"

"I don't have a warrant yet," Dylan reminded him, and fought the smile threatening to lift his mouth.

"Yet?"

Dylan rolled a shoulder. "I have the files now. All of them, right?"

Quade nodded. "Yeah. I can't promise nothing's been copied. But all the originals are there."

"Thanks," Dylan said. "And I have a couple questions for you."

"Shoot."

"Don't tempt me."

Quade laughed. "You have a sense of humor, Deputy. Maybe there's hope for you yet."

"Don't count on it." Dylan balanced his chair on the back legs. "So you found Mrs. Warner?"

"Yes, I did."

"How'd you know she was missing?"

"I might need to take the Fifth on that, considering you haven't made up your mind about a warrant."

"How?"

Quade's dark eyes narrowed. "The guard contacted my private investigator, letting him know that he saw her drive off in a car."

"She was driving?"

"That's what he said. And I found her behind the wheel of the car in her own driveway." He sighed. "But she shouldn't have been driving, she was a mess."

"Where is this guard?"

"I guess he took off, got spooked or something." Quade shrugged. "I suppose, hypothetically speaking, if my investigator could bribe this guard, someone else could, too.''

Dylan nodded. ''Yeah, maybe someone else did.''

''To get my mother out and do what? Frame her for murder?'' He shuddered.

Dylan raised a shoulder and let it drop. ''I don't know. Maybe just to keep us busy elsewhere. But then the sanatorium didn't report her disappearance for hours, while they conducted their own search for her.''

''So who do you suspect?''

Dylan pinched the bridge of his nose and sighed. ''Why didn't I notice the family resemblance before? You're relentless. Don't push. Only Lindsey can get away with that.''

''Don't let her get away, Deputy Dylan.'' He jumped to his feet and straightened his suit. ''Trust me on this. If you care about her at all, keep her and keep her close. You're smarter than I thought and less uptight—you just might be able to handle her.''

Dylan's heart tightened as if his chest was trapped under a tremendous weight. Maybe it was. He wanted to take Quade's advice, but he couldn't be that selfish.

''Don't arrest him!'' Lindsey breathlessly cried as she burst through the door of the police station.

''I'm not arresting him,'' Dylan grumbled. ''I should, but I don't have time for the paperwork.''

Lindsey lifted her chin, and her dark eyes danced with the light of battle. Dylan's pulse kicked into overdrive with anticipation.

''You know the judge would never grant you an

arrest warrant, and you don't want to look like a fool." She smirked.

Dylan smiled and patted the box on his desk. "Looks like I have enough evidence right here to get that arrest warrant. Don't push me, Lindsey."

"That's seems to be his threat du jour," Quade commented with a smile of his own, which expressed his delight in Dylan being on the defensive.

"Don't push you?" Lindsey huffed. "Don't push you? Who's been pushing since the day we met again, Dylan Matthews?"

"That would be you." He rose from the chair and stalked around the front of his desk. To truly appreciate Lindsey's explosive energy, he had to be close enough to touch her.

She pressed a finger to his chest. "Wrong. That would be you!"

"I'll just leave you two kids to hash this out...." Quade took a few side steps toward the door.

Dylan covered Lindsey's mouth with the palm of his hand, worried for a moment if she'd bite, and called out to her brother. "Wait. I want you to look at something first."

"Muzzling her? Do you think that's wise?" He lifted a brow as he retraced his steps to Dylan's desk.

Dylan slowly drew his hand away from her lips.

"What?" she snarled. "Showing him a display of brute force? Police brutality? Macho—"

Dylan pressed a quick kiss to her lips, knowing that was the most effective way of shutting her up. Then, with a shaking hand, he pulled a file from under the box on his desk. He flipped it open and handed it to

Quade. "Are those the township charts you and Oliver went over for alternative sites for the mall?"

Quade studied them. "Definitely. You can compare my handwriting. See, I made notations here and here." He gestured a few inches above the papers. "Evidence. Of course, my fingerprints are already all over them. You got these from the crime scene, then?"

"And denied having them," Lindsey mumbled as she rose on tiptoe to peer over her brother's shoulder.

Dylan didn't bother to contradict her. For her own safety, it was better she didn't know everything.

"You don't trust me," she muttered. "Afraid you were going to see this in print, too? I was seriously trying to help you, stupid me. And you were holding out, keeping stuff back from the press."

"Lindsey." Dylan sighed. "Come on. This is a police investigation. You know how that goes."

"I know I got more information from officers in Chicago than the man I'm sleeping with here in Winter Falls. Yeah, I know how it goes." And she strode out of the office.

"You're not going after her?" Quade handed the folder back.

Dylan tossed the file on his desk and ran his hand over his face. "I should just let her go again."

"Again?"

"This is an old argument," Dylan grumbled. "Aw, hell…"

Quade's mocking laughter followed him as he slammed the door of the police department behind his back. Lindsey had her hand on the door to the diner, two buildings down. "Lindsey!"

She glanced up but pulled open the door.

"Come on!" he said as he caught up with her. "Don't drown your sorrows in black coffee and cinnamon rolls."

"I have no sorrows to drown," she said with a shrug. "I missed lunch today, and I'm hungry."

"You're always hungry. Let's talk about this, privately." He grabbed her free hand and tugged her around on the sidewalk. He led her away from Marge's Diner, toward the outskirts of Winter Falls' city limits.

Lindsey dragged her feet beside him. "I thought you were tired of talking," she said softly.

Dylan shivered. He'd not stopped to grab his jacket, and a brisk autumn breeze blew. Leaves scattered on the sidewalk and landed in the street.

Lindsey wore a sweater, a fuzzy red turtleneck that lovingly embraced her curves. Dylan remembered doing that himself the night before. He wasn't so cold anymore.

Even if she intended to leave town, she deserved more from the man she'd given so much to. "I'm sorry," he began.

"What? What was that?" Lindsey halted in front of the bank and dramatically cocked her ear toward him.

Dylan kept walking, tugging her along with him. "You heard me."

She stumbled into his side, and Dylan caught her close. "You deserve to hear it again," he admitted, and pulled her into his arms in front of her father's newspaper building. "I'm sorry." He lightly kissed the angry-looking bruise on her forehead. Of course, she was too stubborn to leave the gauze on the wound.

He sighed and hugged her closer. "I'm sorry for dragging you through town when you have a concussion."

"They couldn't prove that," she murmured into his shirtfront. "You're only sorry for dragging me through town?"

Dylan rubbed his hands up and down the softness of her sweater-covered back. "No, you know I mean more than that. I'm just— Okay, I really didn't keep much from you."

Lindsey shoved her arms between them and created a wedge of space. Her dark eyes narrowed on his face. "Much?"

Dylan slid his hand into his hair. "I really shouldn't tell you this. This is a police investigation. We're in front of the very reason why I shouldn't tell you anything."

Lindsey tilted her head over her shoulder. "Jeez, the *Gazette*." She caught his hand and pulled him farther down the sidewalk, past the old brick-and-frame buildings that had stood the test of time, even beyond the new buildings with their bright awnings.

She stopped by the wrought-iron fence of the Winter Falls cemetery. Dylan wished she'd kept walking even though his muscles protested with aches from his strenuous run of the previous evening.

He caught her hand before she could reach for the gate. "Let's just stand here."

She raised a brow at him. "Superstitious?"

Dylan watched a crimson leaf fall from an ancient oak just inside the fence. When it drifted to the sidewalk, he tagged it with the toe of his boot. "We've gone far enough. Your father can't see us here."

"You think that's why I wouldn't stay in front of the newspaper building? That I'm hiding you?" A small smile curved her sassy mouth.

Dylan shrugged. "I know your father doesn't approve of me. He knows I've put you in danger. He's right."

"I just didn't want to be by the paper right now," she admitted with a sigh.

Dylan slid a finger down her cheek to the corner of her mouth. The smile was gone. "Why not?"

"He wants me to take it over. He wants to concentrate on Mom now. He wants to help her over this. He thinks he didn't do enough for her before...."

Dylan nodded. "And you're not staying."

"I don't know."

"You said—"

"I know. I know. And I got a call today. The paper in Chicago wants me back. They fired him."

Dylan laughed. He didn't need to ask who "him" was. "Feel good?"

She laughed, too. "Yeah, feels pretty good."

"It would make it sweeter to take his job while he's out there pounding the pavement looking for another one." Dylan fought to keep his tone light. But his heart was so heavy with dread, he could hardly catch a breath.

She was leaving. He'd known it, but it still hurt to think of his life without her. How empty it would be again.

"Yeah, well, I thought about that."

Dylan nodded. "Of course. So you told them yes." He could even imagine her little victory dance after she hung up the phone. Her ego saved. He couldn't blame her for rejoicing about it.

"Naw. I told them I'd think about it. There's a lot going on here. There are a couple of murders to help you solve. My mom to think about…" She knocked her boot against his, crushing the leaf underneath the rubber sole.

"She's doing better, then?"

Lindsey shrugged. "Not according to Evan. I haven't seen her yet. My next stop is the private hospital where Evan took her."

She shivered, and Dylan struggled with the need to hold her again. To tuck her head under his chin and protect her from all her struggles.

He squeezed the bridge of his nose. He was the last person capable of protecting her from anything. "Well, I've got to get back to the department. Your brother dropped off that box…."

"And identified those charts."

"They weren't at the crime scene. I didn't lie to you about that."

"But you've lied to me about other things?"

"Damn it, Lindsey. Can you stop being so difficult for once?"

She shook her head. "'Fraid not. 'Difficult' is what I do best. Where'd you find the charts?"

Dylan rubbed his hand over his chin, the stubble biting into his palm. "I really don't feel—"

"Like you can trust me. Yeah, we've already established that." She spun away, but Dylan caught her arm.

"I don't feel that it's significant. I found them in the sheriff's desk. At his house. In the den where I've been sleeping."

"And you don't think he'd kill a man and then be stupid enough to leave evidence where you'd find it?" Lindsey was astute. He'd known that ten years ago. "I could play devil's advocate."

"You could."

"I could say that he wouldn't suspect you'd go through his desk, that he would never believe you could suspect him."

"I thought of that," Dylan conceded. "I got a search warrant when I found out he was trustee of the property."

Lindsey nodded. "Yeah, you would. You think of everything. You think someone else planted them there?"

Dylan shrugged. "I'd like to believe that."

"Who would do that?"

"Someone trying to throw suspicion off himself."

"You don't think Evan—"

"Lindsey—" He never finished the thought. Beyond the gate he glimpsed a dark figure behind an enormous oak. An arm extended. The afternoon sunshine, sneaking through the trees, bounced off the barrel of a gun.

"Get down!" he shouted, but he didn't wait for Lindsey to comply. He knocked her to the sidewalk with his body, covering her just as the first shots fired. A branch snapped from the tree overhead, raining leaves and twigs on them, as shot after shot rang out.

He drew his weapon from the holster under his arm, but he couldn't leave Lindsey.

"Go! Go!" she urged, her lips moving with the words against his neck.

The firing stopped. Dylan acted before the gun could be reloaded. He leaped to his feet and vaulted over the wrought-iron gate, a spire snagging the leg of his uniform as he cleared it and entered the cemetery.

Chapter Fourteen

Lindsey couldn't draw a breath as she listened for the popping sounds of more gunfire. "Dylan," she whispered as fervently as a prayer on a lonely night. "Be safe."

Her heart hammered wildly against her ribs, but no sounds rang out from inside the cemetery except for the whine of the wind through the trees and the rustling of falling leaves.

She rolled from her back to her side and lay her cheek against the concrete of the sidewalk, feeling the bite of it against her skin. Beneath her sweater, she ran her fingers over the scrape against the curve of her spine. She'd have more bruises in a while. But Dylan had saved her life...again.

"Dylan," she said louder, and she rolled to her stomach to rise up on her knees. Then she reached her trembling hands toward the fence and struggled to her shaky legs.

She caught the top of the gate as she walked through it, and her hand came away with blood. But it wasn't her blood. She was bruised, not scratched.

Dylan had seen to her safety. But had he taken a

bullet for her? He'd completely covered her body with his.

"Dylan!" She screamed his name now and ran down the path through the grave markers and statuary. "Dylan!"

Behind another massive oak, she caught the glow of his golden hair in the afternoon sun. He stood over a grave, his expression stunned as he stared down at it.

Her rubber soles were silent on the asphalt path as she trotted up to him. She had to touch his arm to gain his attention. "Are you all right?"

He didn't even look at her, didn't look up. "I'm fine, fine."

She looked down, too, at the shell casings lying amid the leaves and fresh flowers on a grave. The stone drew her gaze next, and she saw the letters. "Steve Mars."

Dylan shuddered. "The shooter stood here."

She nodded. "Yeah. It wasn't Steve Mars. He's dead, Dylan. I'm not superstitious."

Dylan expelled a ragged breath. "I know. I know he's dead. I'm not superstitious, either."

"Who is it, Dylan? You saw him?"

He shook his head. "No. No, the shooter was gone before I ever made it through the gate."

"But you know who it is. Tell me," she pleaded.

Dylan turned away from the grave of his brother's killer, and his blue eyes were intense but indecipherable. "I don't know. It doesn't make sense."

"What doesn't? Tell me," she insisted.

He shook his head. "I can't say for sure. There are too many suspects, Lindsey, and not enough proof."

She could read the conviction in the tension of his firmly set jaw. He knew. "You're sure you're not hurt?" She raised her bloodied hand.

He caught it quickly in his. "You're hurt!"

"No."

He smeared the blood on his fingertip. Then he touched the back of his thigh. His hand came away with more blood.

"You've been shot!" She leaned down and examined the tear in the back of his uniform and the flesh of his leg.

"Damn gate!"

"You need medical attention."

"I need to get that rookie Jones out here with an evidence bag. I have an investigation to handle."

Lindsey nodded. He didn't want her help anymore. He'd discovered on his own what he needed to know. He didn't need her. No one ever had. She hated the insipid surge of self-pity.

"Do you want—" But she wasn't able to finish.

A police car, with sirens wailing, lurched to a stop at the cemetery gate.

"I'll tell him where you are." She started toward the street. But she turned back to find Dylan staring once again at the grave of Steve Mars.

She threw her arms around him and pressed a quick, soft kiss to his lips. "Thank you! I don't know if I have ever thanked you. You've saved my life so many times now."

He shook his head. "Don't thank me, Lindsey."

"I know. You're just doing your job." She pulled back, but he caught her chin before she could turn away again.

He rubbed one finger over her cheek. She fought to hold in a tear from falling on it.

"Don't, Lindsey. Don't think I'm some kind of hero. I'm nobody's hero. I'm the worst thing that's ever happened to you. I'm worse than a bruised ego and stinging pride. I could cost you your life."

She pressed a finger over his lips. "You saved my life, Dylan. You are a hero, whether you admit it or not."

"Promise me something."

She lifted a brow. "What?"

"Stay safe. Don't be alone with anyone. Watch out for yourself."

"I've got you to do that for me, Dylan. Should I wait for Jones? You do have him following me?"

His fingers slid over her cheek and into her hair. He pressed his lips to hers in a gentle kiss. "Your safety is my biggest concern."

DYLAN'S STOMACH GROWLED in sync with the elevator music playing in his ear while he waited on hold. A glance out the window confirmed night had fallen. He'd missed dinner. Heck, he'd missed lunch, too. And he couldn't even remember breakfast.

But he could remember Lindsey's face, the scrape on the milky skin of her cheek from the sidewalk outside the cemetery. And he cringed when he imagined the bruises on her back from his shoving her to the concrete. He'd hurt her again.

All he could ever do was hurt her. He had nothing to offer her but pain. Good thing she was leaving. Once he wrapped up this murder investigation, she'd head out of town. He'd accepted that.

Despite the ache in his heart, he smiled over the thought of that bastard who'd dumped her reading her byline where his had been. Being vindictive had its merit. And then it didn't. Two men had died because of vindictiveness.

The music stopped, and another confirmation sounded in his ear.

"Thanks for staying over, for getting this done. It's vital," he said into the receiver before replacing it on the desk.

Then he leaned over to dig more files from the box Evan Quade had brought in earlier. Hours ago. He'd been busy, getting shot at, almost getting the woman he loved killed. He was so careless.

And she thought he was a hero. How could such a smart woman be so wrong? He shook his head and pushed his chair back to thumb through another file.

The pieces were adding up. It wouldn't be long now.

LINDSEY KNELT BEFORE her mother's chair and took her scarred hand between both of hers. "Hi, Mom. How are you doing?" The guilt clawed its way through her.

She'd not loved her mother enough, not cared enough about what she'd become. Retha Warner appeared childlike despite her graying hair. The overstuffed chair enveloped her fragile body. Lindsey drank in the sight of her, the simplicity, the sweetness, and something new—the peace.

Perhaps she should call Dylan, tell him her mother had had a miraculous recovery. She would be lucid enough to question now. She sighed and tasted him on her lips. Dylan would have to wait.

Lindsey struggled with the truth in her heart but finally allowed it free. She'd hated this woman. She'd hated her for making Lindsey "that poor Warner girl." Because she'd not been able to forgive the town for gossiping about and pitying her, she'd harbored the biggest grudge against the woman who'd made all the rumors possible.

"I'm sorry, Mom," Lindsey said softly, and pressed a kiss to her mother's hand. "I'm sorry."

"For what, honey? You're always such a good girl."

Lindsey smiled. "I like you believing that, but it's not true. I've been mad at you, Mom, and I had no right to that anger."

Retha leaned forward and patted her daughter's head. "You have every right to your anger, dear. It's kept you strong. Self-pity and despair, they weaken you. I know that. And I failed you. You should be angry with me."

Lindsey shook her head. "You have a right to self-pity and despair. They stole your baby."

A single tear trailed down Retha's scarred cheek, but a small smile curved her mouth. "But he's back. He's a man now. I have to remember that. There's so much I have to remember."

Lindsey glanced around the beautifully appointed

private psychiatric hospital. Evan had spared no expense. A private nurse sat on a chair near the door, and Evan had just left. "You'll remember. You'll get better here. Evan will see to that. I wish I could have helped you."

"You did. You saved my life. I remember the fire."

"You don't need to talk about it," Lindsey assured her. She didn't want to think about that day. "It was a long time ago."

Retha pulled her hand from Lindsey's and touched her scarred cheek. "Not for me. Sometimes it's like it never happened. I don't remember it. And sometimes I remember too much."

"You were terribly depressed. It's all right. I know you didn't really want to hurt yourself."

Retha's dark eyes widened. "What? You think I set the fire?"

"You were home alone, Mom."

"But I wasn't alone."

"But, Mom, I was there. There was only you in the house," Lindsey insisted. She could smell the smoke again, feel the heat and the urgency to find her mother.

Retha shook her head. "Maybe then I was alone. But before that I was not alone."

Lindsey glanced over at the nurse, but the woman merely shrugged. "Then who, Mom? Who was with you?"

"Ask Marge."

DYLAN PULLED OPEN THE door to Marge's Diner.

"I'm closed," she called out from behind the

counter. Then the petite woman glanced up. "You look beat, honey. What can I get you?"

Dylan paused to inhale the rich aroma of strong coffee and cinnamon mixed with the smell of chicken. The smells of home. This place was as much home as the house that had burned to the ground less than a week ago. Maybe it was more so.

"What's cooking?" He slid wearily onto a stool at the counter.

Marge smiled. "Tonight's special was chicken à la king. I might have a plate in the back. And I started some cinnamon rolls for morning. You interested?"

Dylan shook his head and ran a hand through his hair. "Cinnamon rolls are Lindsey's weakness, not mine. Got any pie around?"

Marge snorted. "Have I got pie? You were gone a long time, Dylan. Too long."

"Maybe it wasn't long enough. Maybe I shouldn't have come back." He cupped his hands around the mug she filled for him. But the heat emanating through the ceramic did nothing to warm him.

"You had to come back, Dylan. There was a lot of unfinished business here." She slapped a piece of peach pie in front of him.

"Unfinished? Enough people died ten years ago, Marge."

"Too many."

"Yes."

"So you serious about that girl?" she asked, ever the busybody.

Dylan shrugged. "Serious about Lindsey? What

would be the point? She's leaving.''

Marge shook her head. "She won't leave Winter Falls, not now, not ever.''

Dylan shivered. "Her old paper already asked her back. She has a job there, a life there. There's nothing for her here.''

"You're here.''

"And I haven't figured out why.''

"Unfinished business again, Dylan. It comes back to that. Eat up.''

She held the coffeepot near his untouched mug.

Dylan waved a hand. "It's late. I should be going. Why don't you wrap this up for me, and I'll take it back to my motel.''

Marge raised her chin. "It's not that late. I was here alone. Go ahead and eat. I like the company.''

"No. I'll just take it with me.''

"Where, Dylan?''

Dylan slid his hand over the gun on his holster. "I already said, Marge.''

"I know what you said. Why don't you just eat up while we discuss this unfinished business?''

"Marge.'' Dylan sighed. "I know why.''

"You know Steve Mars was my baby?'' The older woman's eyes filled with tears. "And you killed him.''

Dylan shook his head. "I didn't kill him, Marge. He killed himself.''

"You're lying. Always such a liar, Deputy Matthews. But the sheriff protected you, as he always has. You've been a free man the last ten years while my son has been in the ground.'' Her face, usually so attractive, twisted into a mask of hatred and madness.

"So you waited for me to come home? Then you decided to settle the score?''

"I didn't know for sure that Steve was my son. I suspected.'' She smiled. "He had my mother's eyes. I tried to get the records from Chet's office. But he always engaged his alarm. He really safeguarded his secrets. But when his idiot nephew took over, well, I saw my chance. He forgot one night. But I didn't.''

"You took the records from Chet's office? The adoption records?''

She nodded, then laughed. "I know Evan Quade is Retha's son. She's too crazy to ever realize it, though.''

Dylan fought a shudder. "After you learned the truth, you schemed?''

"Yes, everyone had to pay. I offered them hospitality, gave them food and fake smiles, while I plotted their deaths. You were going to be hard. I knew that.''

"You tried a few times.''

She laughed, and the sound echoed eerily in the empty restaurant. "Those weren't tries. I didn't want you dead yet. I knew you'd get out of the fire. And the gunshots were never close.'' She patted her hair. "I'm an excellent shot. I wanted you alive, like this. I wanted to talk to you. I have something for you, you know.''

"The letter from Steve.''

She laughed again. "The letter you made him write. Did you force him to pen those lies just before you killed him? You must have.''

"Let me see the letter, Marge," Dylan urged. Under the edge of the counter, he held his gun across his knees. He didn't want to hurt her. This woman had been hurt enough.

She pulled a folded paper from her apron pocket. "He didn't say those things. Those are your words."

Dylan took the letter from her shaking fingers.

Dear Dylan,
I'm so sorry about Jimmy's death. To protect my sister, I didn't speak of my reasons for killing him, but I feel I must let you know now. You will be an uncle soon. Jimmy compromised my sister, and instead of owning up to his responsibilities, he laughed. He was never half the man you are. I know that you will help Sarah raise her child, that you will offer the moral guidance that Jimmy and myself are unable to provide. Because I was raised in a secure, loving home, I know that the defect that caused me to put the knife in Jimmy's back is genetic. Because of this, I know there is no hope for my future. I am a danger to others, and I don't deserve to live. Please express my love and apologies to all.

Steve

"Lies!" Marge hissed. "Lies. Genetic defect. He means my genes! You mean my genes. He wouldn't have said that. He wouldn't have written those lies. You made him do it!"

"He killed Jimmy." Dylan closed the door on that

old question and realized that his instincts had been wrong all those years ago. But not this time.

"And you killed him!"

"He killed himself, Marge. He killed himself. Read those lines. That's Steve's handwriting, Steve's words. He gave this letter to Chet Oliver before his death, had to have been at his sentencing. You killed innocent people, Marge. Chet and the mayor had done their jobs. Steve wasn't angry. He was sorry." He tried to reach for her hand, but she jerked away from the counter.

"No!" Her shout bounced off the walls. "You think it's ended? You think I'm going to accept that? It's too late, you know...."

Dylan drew a quick breath. "Marge, nobody else has to get hurt. Come with me now."

She laughed and shook her head. "You think I'm crazy? You think I'm going to let you hang me in that jail cell like you hung my son? You're not taking me anywhere. I'm taking you."

Dylan lifted the gun above the counter. "Marge, I have to place you under arrest."

Her hysterical laughter rang out. "You think you have backup? That rookie cop parked behind the building?"

His heart jumped. Jones was supposed to be watching Lindsey. "Jones? You did something to Jones? I talked to him just a little while ago." And he'd been parked in the lot of a private psychiatric hospital, not Marge's.

"I brought him a cinnamon roll and a cup of coffee."

Dylan cursed. He'd told the kid to stay with Lindsey, to not let her out of his sight.

"You killed him?" He stood up and edged down the counter toward the back door. Before he made it a few steps, his foot hit something. He glanced down at Lindsey's leather backpack, lying on the floor next to a booth.

"Where's Lindsey?" His heart beat so fiercely it shook his chest.

Marge smiled again. "Those rolls and coffee are her weakness, Dylan. She had some questions for me. We had quite a talk over coffee and rolls."

"Where is she?" Panic streaked through his stomach. He glanced down at the bag again and noted that a cinnamon roll had rolled out of it and onto the shiny linoleum.

"And you know, it's too late for the sheriff, too. I sent him something special. Had Will bring it up to him for me. You'd let Will through to see him, wouldn't you?"

Dylan shook his head. "What if Will had some himself? Do you want to hurt Lindsey's father, too? If you hurt her, you know it'll kill him?"

"He cost me a child. He deserves to lose her," she said of her lover.

"What?"

"You never asked who fathered my child? William Warner was my high school sweetheart. When I got pregnant, I didn't tell him. I didn't want to derail his dreams of college. I let him go away, and I went away, too. Everyone thought I went to Paris. I just went a few miles down the road and had a baby boy.

I met Retha there. And then that tramp goes away to college, and she comes back with my lover as her husband. He should have been my husband!''

"None of that has anything to do with Lindsey. She never hurt you!"

"Little bitch treated me like the other woman for years. Treated me like I was beneath her. Her mother was the other woman. Will was mine! He was the father of my child.''

Dylan kept the gun trained on her. "Where is she, Marge? Tell me now!"

"It's too late for her, Dylan. I want you to see her hanging like I saw my son hanging that night."

"You were at the jail. You were talking to me out front when Steve used the tie he'd kept after his sentencing...." Dylan remembered. "You know I didn't do it. You were there. I thought he'd been searched when he was returned to the holding cell."

Marge shook her head, tears springing from her eyes and falling like rain on the countertop. "No. You killed him. You hung him and then you stood out front, talking to me, just as calmly as I've been talking to you, while he died."

"Oh, my God!" Dylan vaulted over the counter and pushed open the door to the kitchen. Nothing hung from the rafters but pots and pans. "Where, Marge?

"Marge!" Before he could turn around a shot rang out over his labored breaths, shattering the quiet of the diner.

Chapter Fifteen

The coarse fibers of rope bit into Lindsey's neck and constricted each breath she struggled to inhale. But the noose could have been tighter and would be tighter if she lost her grip.

She should have fought her, but the gun had never been far from Lindsey's face. A twitch of Marge's finger, and Lindsey would have been gone. She'd figured her chances were better if she went along with Marge's plan and slipped the pre-tied noose around her neck. The crazy woman thought Lindsey had calmly drunk her drugged coffee and eaten the doctored roll.

Well, a plant at the diner would need resuscitation soon, but not Lindsey. Not if she could keep hold of the branch from which she currently swung. Her nails scraped against the bark as she struggled to tighten her hold on the ancient oak.

Fortunately, Marge had made her climb the tree and tie the rope around the branch herself.

''It'll be a lot less painful than a gunshot wound, Lindsey,'' she'd promised. ''You'll just fall asleep and let go of the branch. You'll not feel any pain. You'll just fall asleep.''

Lindsey had wanted to snort at her in victory. She'd figured that after Marge left she'd be able to untie the rope and jump down. Then she'd run for Dylan.

But Marge hadn't waited for her to fall asleep. She'd grabbed her leg and pulled her down.

Lindsey hadn't lost her grip on the branch with her hands. And with her legs she'd kicked out at the crazy woman. ''Shoot me then, you psycho!''

Marge had laughed. ''I don't need to shoot you, sweetie. I just have to let the drugs work. You'll fall asleep soon. You'll let go of the tree. Holding up your weight will be very tiring.'' Then she'd walked toward the cemetery gate and Winter Falls.

Her grip on the tree slipped a bit. She whimpered, her arms burning from the exertion of holding up her weight.

With an erratically pounding heart, she struggled to secure her hold on the branch. A bit more slack evaporated between the noose around her neck and the length of rope tied around the tree. She fought down the panic and steadied her breaths.

She could breathe. The rope wasn't in a stranglehold around her neck. All she had to do was keep her grip on the tree. Hang on, instead of hang.

That lunatic was out there somewhere in the darkness. The streetlight barely reached beyond the gate of the cemetery. And Steve Mars's grave was farther down the path, behind the oak from which Lindsey hung.

Marge could be out there. Or worse, she could be

going after Dylan. Lindsey figured she was the bait. Marge intended to lure him to the cemetery and kill him on Steve Mars's grave.

"Okay," she whispered, her voice fading in and out with the constriction of the rope. "Okay, she has to set the trap. She can't be here now. She'd go to the station or back to the diner. She can't be here."

She could kill him at the station. Who else would be working so late? Dylan would be alone, looking for his evidence to imprison the killer. He thought he knew who it was, but would he have ever suspected Marge?

Lindsey thought he'd been leaning toward the sheriff despite his claims to the contrary. If not for her mother's ramblings and a quick check with her brother's copies of the records from Arborview, Lindsey would have never thought Marge capable of killing.

But Dylan had the originals from Arborview. He'd planned to go through them. If he didn't know now, he'd know soon.

Lindsey glanced up at the few stars she could spy through the branches of the tree. No wind blew, but a few leaves still drifted down onto her and the grave below her dangling feet.

Why hadn't she paid more attention in gymnastics? Despite the forced levity of her thought, tears stung her eyes. She couldn't swing her leg up on the branch again.

And why did she wear such tight jeans? There was no way. Every attempt loosened her tentative grip.

And the muscles in her arms burned with the effort of holding up her weight.

She had to keep talking, even though every word stuck in her constricted throat. The silence of the cemetery was too unnerving, more so than the noose around her neck. And while her reporter's brain formed more questions, she was too scared to ask them. What if someone or something answered?

Bark edged beneath her nails, biting into the quick. She welcomed the discomfort; it kept her alert.

Because of the quiet of the night, she heard the gunshot. It was far off. Just a pop of sound in the stillness. But she knew what it was. Thanks to Marge, she'd gotten quite familiar with the sound of gunshots.

"Dylan!" she screamed as loud as she could, a mere croak.

She couldn't let that crazy bitch win. Lindsey glanced at the branch again. If she could drag the rope down toward the thinner part, perhaps she could work the knot, or perhaps the branch would snap under her weight.

She struggled, using her nails under the edge of the rope, digging into it and the bark of the tree. A twig snapped, but too many protruded from the branch, preventing the rope from budging.

What if Dylan was shot? What if his life bled out of him? What would she do in a world without Dylan? She had to get to him!

"Okay, Lindsey," she panted. She could do this. She had to get a better grasp on the tree.

She skimmed one hand farther up the thick branch, bark scraping the tender skin of her palm. Now the other one. She wiggled, got her legs to swing and scooted the other hand up, so that she could lock her fingers over the top, near the rope.

She dragged in a breath, rubbed the skin of her neck against the stinging fibers of the rope, and then she swung her legs again.

Dylan. She had to get to Dylan. He'd saved her so many times. It was her turn to save him.

The swing of her legs jerked the rest of her body. Her fingers slipped free of one another. Her hands slipped from the branch, and her neck snapped as the last of the slack left the rope. And she swung.

AT A DEAD RUN, Dylan crashed through the cemetery gate. The pounding of his footfalls on the asphalt path echoed through the dense trees, cement statuary and marble tombstones.

Lindsey had to be here. Beside her son's grave would be the place Marge would choose to wreak the last of her vengeance. Dylan rounded the path and passed the ancient oak just as a slice of the moon shifted from behind some clouds. Light shone through the branches and onto the silhouette of a hanging woman.

''God, please, no!'' he raged. He couldn't shut off the flood of emotions. The pain nearly brought him to his knees.

Her feet weren't that far from the ground. He reached for her, lifted her, and a gurgle of air slipped through her parted lips.

From his pocket he grabbed his Swiss Army knife and managed to swing it high enough to catch the rope above her head. The blade gnawed at the thick fibers one at a time until finally the rope broke apart, half hanging from the tree, the other half still a noose around the neck of the woman he loved.

Fighting down panic, he dropped to the ground with her in his arms. He puffed a couple of breaths into her mouth while his fingers struggled with the knot at the base of her neck.

"Lindsey, are you all right? Can you breathe?"

Her dark eyes blinked open, her stare disturbingly unfocused.

"Please, God!" He shuddered. Then he sealed her nose and puffed a few more breaths into her mouth.

Her arms circled his shoulders, and her lips moved under his. "Umm," she moaned. Then she gasped for a breath.

"Lindsey," Dylan murmured as he ran his fingers over her precious face and into her hair. "Lindsey."

She coughed. "We have to…get out of here. Trap. She's here…with a gun. Dangerous. Marge…"

Although her voice was no louder than a rasp, he caught her panicked words. "I know it was Marge. It was, Lindsey."

"The shot… You shot her?"

He shook his head. "No, I didn't shoot her."

"Then Jones—"

"Is taking a long nap tonight. No, it wasn't Jones. Marge."

"She…" Lindsey shuddered in his arms. "She shot herself."

Running footsteps on the asphalt path echoed

around the oak tree. A voice rang out from the darkness. "I think I see them!"

"Over here," Dylan called out.

Evan Quade and Will Warner halted abruptly next to Dylan and Lindsey. Will dropped to his knees. "Sweetheart, you're all right?"

Lindsey nodded. "I'm fine, Dad. Marge—"

"I'm so sorry, honey." He ran his hands over her face. "I should have known. I should have seen—"

"Nobody did," Dylan interrupted, and put a hand on Will's shoulder.

The older man shuddered, and a sob bubbled out of him. "But—"

"No buts, Dad," Lindsey rasped, and struggled to her knees. She threw her arms around her father.

Evan Quade choked out a breath. "Damn, Dylan, you're fast. I lost you by the diner. Then Will stopped me. We couldn't figure out where you went."

Dylan turned to him. "It was a guess."

"A good guess. Oh, my God!" Evan staggered back a couple of steps. He gestured toward the tree. "She hung you, Lindsey? We have to get you to a hospital. How long—how can you be alive?"

"I wondered that, too," Dylan admitted. "Marge toyed with me a long time before she…"

"Took you…long enough," Lindsey griped in a whisper. "Held the branch…lost my grip…"

Lindsey wilted in her father's arms, her head lolling against his shoulder, the noose still around her neck.

Evan called for an ambulance on his cell phone. And Dylan took her from her father's arms. "She's breathing. She's just fainted."

"That's going to tick her off," Evan said.

"I'll carry her to the street...." Before he turned for the asphalt path, Dylan glanced up at the ancient oak where the frayed piece of rope still hung. Where Lindsey had hung... Because of him.

"SO YOU'RE HERE in an official capacity," Lindsey said a couple of hours later from the gurney in the hospital emergency room. Despite being groggy from the painkiller they'd given her, she spotted the notepad in his hand and the detached expression on his face.

This was not the same man who'd held her in his arms in the cemetery. This was not her lover. This was Deputy Dylan Matthews.

"I need to get all the facts, so I can complete the report." His blue gaze never touched on her face, wouldn't meet her eyes.

Lindsey yawned.

"Can't this wait till morning?" Evan asked from behind Dylan. He held out a coffee cup to Lindsey.

She smiled and grasped the foam cup in both trembling, bandaged hands.

"Is caffeine really a good idea right now?" Dylan asked.

Lindsey smiled again. Perhaps he cared a little bit. "If you intend to interrogate me, it is."

"I don't intend to interrogate you," Dylan grumbled. "I just have a few questions. I want to know what Marge said to you."

Because of the bandages and painkillers, she couldn't feel a thing physically. Emotionally she felt too much. "I had some questions to ask her. She insisted I have a cup of coffee and a cinnamon roll while she answered them."

"Ever the reporter," Dylan commented. "What kind of questions?"

"I wanted to know why she tried to kill my mother."

"What?" His blue eyes widened.

"Yeah, chalk another one up to her. Marge started the fire that scarred my mother. She was with Mom before the fire started. My mother told me that tonight. Before I went to see her, I checked through some copies of Arborview records."

Dylan glared at her brother. "Wonder where she got her hands on those."

Evan laughed and sipped at his own cup of coffee.

"So you figured it out?" Dylan asked her.

"Of course," Lindsey scoffed.

"So you know Steve Mars was your brother?"

"What!" She nearly dropped her cup. Dylan took it from her nerveless fingers. "What are you talking about?"

"I guess Marge didn't answer many of your questions."

"No." Lindsey shivered. "No, she was too busy trying to poison me. I have a brother. He's right there."

Dylan didn't glance at Evan now. "Your father and Marge were high school sweethearts. She was pregnant when he left for college. She didn't want to derail his dreams. She went to Arborview before he went away. That's where she met your mother the first time. The second time was when Retha came here as your father's bride.''

"So that's why she tried to kill my mother.''

"And not just the fire,'' Dylan said. "I believe she was giving your mother drugs during her visits to her. Probably put them in the food she brought her. She wanted your mother incapacitated.''

"Because she wanted my father.''

"And your father was too stupid to see it,'' Will Warner said from the doorway. He leaned wearily against the jamb. "So Steve Mars was my son?''

Dylan nodded. "So Marge claimed.''

"We were close.'' Will sighed. "If I hadn't met Retha while I was at college, I may have come home to marry Marge. But I fell for your mother, Lindsey. Even after she got sick, I never stopped loving her. I believed Marge and I were just...''

"She believed more,'' Dylan said. "Then Steve killed Jimmy for getting Sarah pregnant. He didn't intend to help her. He laughed when Steve asked his intentions regarding her pregnancy. Later Steve killed himself in the holding cell. He wrote me a letter during the sentencing.''

Lindsey said, "I'd like to see it, Dylan.''

He shook his head. "I need it for evidence.''

She wanted to argue with him, but her head ached.

"And?'' Evan prompted.

"And Marge believed all these years that I killed Steve. I don't think she ever accepted he killed Jimmy. She blamed the sheriff, Chet Oliver and the mayor, who was then the judge, for her son's pleading guilty. She didn't know for sure that Steve was hers until she stole the records from Chet's office. Then she waited until I came home to start exacting her revenge.''

Lindsey's heart ached, and she reached for his hand. "It's not your fault, Dylan."

Dylan twisted his lips, but the expression in no way resembled a smile. His eyes narrowed on her bandaged hands. "How did she get you to the cemetery?''

Lindsey fought a sigh. "She acted fast. She thought I was going to fall asleep like Jones had in his police car. She told me she was dumping garbage, but she must have brought him a roll. With him following me I thought I was safe. Is he all right?''

Dylan nodded. "He didn't stuff the cinnamon roll in his backpack like you did."

"Or dump coffee in a flowerpot, either, I bet," Lindsey added.

"So she took you out the back door?''

"Yup. She had a gun stuck in my back. She pushed me all the way to the cemetery. I figured she'd try to shoot me there, and I intended to wait for my moment to fight. But she never dropped that gun. She made me slip the noose around my neck.'' She lifted her fingertips to the sore skin at her throat.

She glanced up to see Dylan's gaze focused intently on her neck. His handsome face was grim.

"I'm all right," she insisted to all the worried men in the room.

She continued, "She made me climb the tree, but not far. I figured out why later. She told me to tie the other end of the rope around the branch. Then she tried to convince me how painless hanging would be. She was lying.''

She took a sip of the bitter coffee and grimaced. ''Anyhow, she said I'd just fall asleep and fall off the tree branch. Of course, she didn't know that I wasn't drugged. I figured on waiting till she left, then untying the rope and climbing down. But she jumped up and caught my leg and dragged me down. I still had my hold on the branch. I hung on for a long time.'' She held up her hands. Bandages covered the raw skin. Blood penetrated the gauze. Apparently the painkiller had been a good idea.

''And while you hung from that tree, she toyed with me in the diner. Then when I looked for you in the back room, she shot herself.''

Lindsey guessed he blamed himself for that, too. She suspected that Marge's final revenge was for Dylan to live with the guilt of all those deaths. Lindsey's, too. ''None of this was your fault, Dylan. She must have seen that at the end. Had she read the letter from Steve?''

''She thought I forced him to write it.''

''She tried to convince herself of that, but I'm sure she knew the truth. That's why she shot herself instead of you.'' She reached for his hand again, but he took a step back, nearly bumping into Evan's coffee cup.

Will Warner settled into a chair on the other side of Lindsey's bed. ''So she killed Chet and the mayor?''

Dylan nodded. ''Yeah, she drugged them with rolls. She didn't wait long enough before she shot

Chet, though, and he struggled. A bullet went into the ceiling. I found the guard from Arborview. He confirmed she got Retha out, probably hoping to frame her. She was more successful drugging the mayor. Then she staged the gas leak.''

''And the fire? It was her.''

Dylan nodded. ''It was all her. She drugged the sheriff, too, knowing he couldn't mix other drugs with his heart meds without bringing on an attack. Tried it again tonight. The rolls she sent with you, Will.''

Will rubbed a hand over his face. ''I nearly ate one. But I brought them here, and your guard at the sheriff's door took them right to the lab.''

''I had her then, so I went to the diner. I think she tried to drug me, too. But it's over now.'' Dylan closed his book and tucked his pen into the wire spiral holding the papers together.

Lindsey suspected he was referring to more than the murder case. When his deep blue eyes settled on her face, she read the regret in them. It was over now.

Chapter Sixteen

Dylan had avoided the cemetery in Winter Falls until that day he and Lindsey had been shot at near the gate. Even after he'd entered it, he'd never ventured where he was now. His family plot.

He stood over the graves of his parents and his brother. This was his legacy. Death. This was all he had to offer. Two nights ago, Lindsey had nearly died because of him. Because Marge had known he loved her.

He glanced over his shoulder at the ancient oak near Steve Mars's grave. Then he rubbed a hand over his face. If he closed his eyes, he could see her swinging from that tree. For two nights, he'd avoided sleep because of the nightmares that plagued him.

What if he'd not found her in time? What if she'd died? A surge of dread poured through his heart, causing it to ache even more. He ached for her. He ached for her upbeat attitude, for her sassy mouth, for her loving arms....

He'd not seen her since that night at the hospital. But she must have come around the police station. This morning an article printed in the *Gazette* referred to Steve's suicide note. Lindsey's headline had proclaimed Rumors Laid to Rest. Officially he was cleared of Steve's death.

He owed her for that. Although there were still some people who couldn't look him in the eye, he could stay in Winter Falls.

He knelt and leaned over the graves to pluck a petal from the roses near his mother's tombstone. The sheriff. He still loved her even though she was gone.

When Lindsey left, he'd still love her, too. He accepted that and accepted that he couldn't ask her to stay. He had nothing to offer her. His legacy was here.

The petal of the red rose was as silky as Lindsey's skin. He lifted it to his nose. And as fragrant.

"Dylan."

He surged to his feet and turned to her, as if thinking of her had conjured her up. "Lindsey."

"Come here often?" she asked with a soft reverence for the dead.

"No. First time, actually. Cowardly of me," he scoffed. "But that's what someone once called me, a coward. I think it fits."

Lindsey chuckled. "Well, admitting it is the first step."

"Accepting it. It's all there is. I'm taking no more steps from here." He sighed. "So did you come here to say goodbye?"

"Goodbye?" Her smile slipped.

"Yeah, you have a job waiting in Chicago. Some gloating, too."

Lindsey shrugged and rubbed her bandaged hands over the sleeves of her turtleneck sweater. "I don't think I ever intended to go back. I already have a job."

"I saw the paper this morning."

She smiled again. "You mad?"

"You bullied Jones into letting you look at that letter." He pushed a hand through his hair and barely stopped himself from reaching for her. "That letter wasn't for the public."

"It needed to be done."

"Rumors laid to rest," he murmured. "I suppose you expect me to thank you."

Lindsey sighed. "I know better than to expect anything from you, Dylan. Wasn't that our deal?"

He couldn't speak now of his deal with her. He'd broken the rules. He'd fallen in love with her.

"But to answer your question, I don't expect your gratitude. I did it to thank you." Her dark eyes filled with emotions. He only allowed himself to see the gratitude.

He raised a brow in confusion. "Why? For what?"

She smiled. "You saved my life. Again. You saved my life again and again. Really, I think Marge had it in for me more than anyone else."

He shook his head. "No. It was me. She used you to get to me."

"I figured I was the bait the other night. She was using me to trap you here." She shivered.

Dylan's arms ached to wrap around her, to hold her close and protect her from the painful memories of that night. Perhaps she was right. Perhaps he needed to make the next step. He'd already admitted he was a coward. Now was the time to be brave. "I don't think she ever intended to kill me."

"You said you thought she'd poisoned you."

"No poison. Tranquilizers. She had a prescription from Arborview. She was an outpatient there. She used them to drug everybody. Of course, the tranquilizers were not compatible with Sheriff Buck's high blood pressure pills. That's what caused his heart attack the night he hit the tree. Marge knew that."

"So Marge was getting psychiatric help?" Lindsey chuckled with a bitter edge. "Guess it didn't help."

The question dawned in her dark eyes. Her reporter's brain had kicked in. "But if she didn't intend to kill you, why kill me?"

Dylan took a quick breath. "Her revenge."

"But how?"

He glanced back at his parents' graves. At Jimmy's. Was it fair? Should he burden her with his legacy? "This is what happens to people I care about." He gestured at the manicured ground.

Lindsey stepped closer. He could feel her heat, feel the brush of her fuzzy sweater against the hair on his forearm. "Their deaths had nothing to do with you."

He shook his head. "I should have tried to stop my dad from driving that night. Mom would be alive."

"You wouldn't have been able to stop him. You were just a child. Your mother shouldn't have gotten in the car with him. She shouldn't have let you in that car."

"You're saying it was her fault?"

"No, but it was more hers than yours. And it was your father's for driving drunk. It wasn't yours."

He smiled sadly over her vehemence. "He knew that. That's why he drank himself to death."

"He was sick."

"He was weak and cowardly." He barked out a bitter laugh. "Who's to say I wouldn't have done the same thing if I'd been too late the other night? If you'd died because of me…"

Despite her bandages, Lindsey grabbed his shoulders and turned him around. "*I'm* to say you wouldn't have, Dylan. I may have teased you about being a coward. But you're not. You're the bravest man I know. You would never be so weak."

He shook his head. "Yeah, you're right. I'd deserve to suffer the rest of my life, as Marge had intended."

"And Jimmy's death. You had nothing to do with that."

"I should have known what kind of man he was. I should have known about Sarah. I should have stopped him."

"Steve was his best friend, and he didn't know. But he stopped him. It was too late, though, and it was wrong. Jimmy didn't deserve to die. Neither did Steve."

Lindsey dropped her hands. "I still can't believe he was my brother. From an only child to having two brothers…"

Dylan touched her cheek, ran one finger over the satiny skin. "Are you okay with that?"

She sighed. "I wish I'd known all my life, but I can handle it."

He smiled. "You can handle anything. I've never met a woman like you. You're so strong, so secure."

She laughed. "You are crazy, Dylan Matthews, if you believe that. I'm the coward."

He shook his head. "You're not. In every dangerous situation, you used your head."

"And nearly lost it. You saved me every time. But you're avoiding my question. I'm a reporter, Deputy. You can't sidetrack me."

"I can't?" he challenged. He slid his finger from her cheek to the curve of her ear and slipped his fingers into the tangle of her glossy curls. He stroked his thumb back and forth over her full lower lip.

Her breath whispered against his skin. He pushed his thumb between her parted lips and shuddered over the brush of her tongue against it. His mouth replaced his thumb. He plunged his tongue between her lips. Hot.

He slid his arms around her and pulled her softness against the tautness of his ready body. Never had he wanted as badly as he wanted her. To keep. Always.

Lindsey pulled back, sliding her mouth along his stubbled chin. "Dylan…"

He gazed into her dark eyes, and he glimpsed hope there. "You're not leaving?"

She shook her head. "No, I have a job here. I love working with my dad."

"And Winter Falls?"

She snorted. "Well, it's Winter Falls. It's small town and gossipy. And it's home."

He nodded. "Yeah, it's home. I guess I'm going

to have to find one of those. I can't stay in a motel forever."

"No, you can't."

He dropped his mouth to hers again, but she dodged his seeking lips. "Dylan…"

"Lindsey." He dragged in a deep breath. "Marge knew something."

"What?" she prodded.

"You're relentless."

"Everybody knows that," she scoffed. "You're awfully evasive, Deputy Matthews. What are you hiding?"

He dragged her closer and tucked her head beneath his chin, where her wayward curls teased his throat. "My love. I'm hiding the fact that I love you."

Her lips curved against his throat. "And why would you do something so silly?"

Reluctantly he released her and turned back to the graves of the people he'd loved before her. "That's why. This is my legacy, Lindsey. I lose the people I love."

"Foolish man. You've already said I'm relentless. You're never going to lose me, not now that you finally admitted I got to you."

"You don't care that I love you?" He raised a brow.

She popped him in the shoulder with a bandaged hand. "I've been working on it for a long while."

"Working on it? And why was that?"

She smiled. "Because I've always loved you. You've always been my hero, Dylan Matthews. Even when I thought I didn't believe in them anymore, you were my hero.''

"Lindsey," he cautioned. "I'm nobody's hero."

Lindsey shook her head. "How many times do you have to save me before I can call you my hero?"

"Let's not put it to the test, okay? How about you save me this time?"

She glanced down at the graves. "I think I already have, but what do you have in mind? Something wicked, I hope." She ran a bandaged hand down his chest.

Dylan smiled. "Actually, something honorable. How about I put a ring on your finger, and you keep it there. Like, I don't know, forever."

"Forever? You want that long an engagement?" Her dark eyes shone with love and humor.

Dylan's heart swelled. "No, I want a very short engagement, but a very long marriage."

She threw her arms around his neck. "Dylan, I love you so much! I always have."

"I don't deserve you, Lindsey, but I intend to work on that…the rest of our lives." He took her mouth in a tender kiss.

Lindsey quickly turned the tenderness into raging passion as she pushed her tongue between his lips and slid it along his. "And you want me? You really want to keep me?"

Dylan understood the question, understood his Lindsey. "I never intend to let you go. I love you so much. Let's go somewhere, so that I can show you how much."

"I moved out of my father's house."

"You have? Where are you staying?"

"There's an apartment above the newspaper. It needed some cleaning. It still needs some decorating. And it's awfully lonely. It needs you, Dylan. I need you, Dylan."

He took her mouth in another deep, tender kiss. Then he turned her toward the gate to the cemetery, and they walked through it arm and arm.

On the other side of the gate stood Sarah Hutchins and her son. "Sarah," Lindsey gasped.

"Your father said you were looking for Dylan here," she said. "You gave me my proof." She gestured with the newspaper she held in one hand. Her eyes misted with tears, and she looked up at Dylan. "I'm sorry. I'm very sorry."

Jeremy Hutchins held his mother's free hand with both of his. His deep blue eyes full of wonder, he whispered, "You're my uncle?"

Moisture stung Dylan's eyes. "Yes, I am."

"Is that your police car at the curb?"

Dylan laughed. "Yes, it is. Would you like to work the siren?"

Eagerly Jeremy nodded, then stopped to ask, "Is it all right, Mom?"

She nodded. "Yes, you'll be spending a lot of time with your uncle from now on."

Dylan took the hand her son dropped before he ran for the police car. "Thank you, Sarah."

She nodded, her lips tight. "It's the right thing to do. I should have done it long ago. I'm sorry."

Before following Jeremy to his car, he caught Lindsey tight. "Thank you."

LINDSEY LAY BACK on the old brass bed in her new apartment. "I like the way you thank me, Deputy."

Dylan kissed his way up her body, dipped his tongue in her navel and swirled it around her nipples. She wasn't so relaxed anymore.

"In fact," she said, "if you thank me anymore, I may not make it."

He drew her nipple into his mouth, and Lindsey felt the pull all the way to her toes. "Dylan."

His fingers slipped inside her, where she pulsed yet with the pleasure he had already brought her. She crested and dug her nails into his back. "Dylan."

"Lindsey," he said. Then he removed his fingers and drove into her, took her over the edge of sanity until all she could do was pant his name as pleasure tore her apart.

Then he joined her in the insanity, chanting her name. "I love you."

She'd never tire of hearing those words. And never tire of saying them back. "I love you." She had a legacy of her own for her lawman, a legacy of love.

A ROYAL MONARCH'S SEARCH FOR AN HEIR LEADS TO DANGER IN:

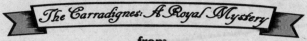
The Carradignes: A Royal Mystery

from
HARLEQUIN®
INTRIGUE®

Plain-Jane royal secretary Ellie Standish wanted one night to shine. But when she was mistaken for a princess and kidnapped by masked henchmen, this dressed-up Cinderella had only one man to turn to—one of her captors: a dispossessed duke who had his own agenda to protect her and who ignited a fire in her soul. Could Ellie trust this man with her life…and her heart?

Don't miss:
THE DUKE'S COVERT MISSION
JULIE MILLER June 2002

And check out these other titles in the series

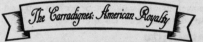
The Carradignes: American Royalty

available from **HARLEQUIN AMERICAN ROMANCE:**

THE IMPROPERLY PREGNANT PRINCESS
JACQUELINE DIAMOND March 2002

THE UNLAWFULLY WEDDED PRINCESS
KARA LENNOX April 2002

THE SIMPLY SCANDALOUS PRINCESS
MICHELE DUNAWAY May 2002

And coming in November 2002:
THE INCONVENIENTLY ENGAGED PRINCE
MINDY NEFF

Available at your favorite retail outlet.

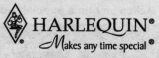
HARLEQUIN®
Makes any time special ®

Visit us at www.eHarlequin.com

HICR

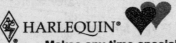

Princes...Princesses...
London Castles...New York Mansions...
To live the life of a royal!

In 2002, Harlequin Books lets you escape to a world of royalty with these royally themed titles:

Temptation:
January 2002—*A Prince of a Guy* (#861)
February 2002—*A Noble Pursuit* (#865)

American Romance:
The Carradignes: American Royalty (Editorially linked series)
March 2002—*The Improperly Pregnant Princess* (#913)
April 2002—*The Unlawfully Wedded Princess* (#917)
May 2002—*The Simply Scandalous Princess* (#921)
November 2002—*The Inconveniently Engaged Prince* (#945)

Intrigue:
The Carradignes: A Royal Mystery (Editorially linked series)
June 2002—*The Duke's Covert Mission* (#666)

Chicago Confidential
September 2002—*Prince Under Cover* (#678)

The Crown Affair
October 2002—*Royal Target* (#682)
November 2002—*Royal Ransom* (#686)
December 2002—*Royal Pursuit* (#690)

Harlequin Romance:
June 2002—*His Majesty's Marriage* (#3703)
July 2002—*The Prince's Proposal* (#3709)

Harlequin Presents:
August 2002—*Society Weddings* (#2268)
September 2002—*The Prince's Pleasure* (#2274)

Duets:
September 2002—*Once Upon a Tiara/Henry Ever After* (#83)
October 2002—*Natalia's Story/Andrea's Story* (#85)

Celebrate a year of royalty with Harlequin Books!

Available at your favorite retail outlet.

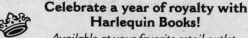

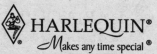

HARLEQUIN®
Makes any time special ®

Visit us at www.eHarlequin.com

HSROY02

MONTANA *Bred*

From the bestselling series

MONTANA MAVERICKS

Wed in Whitehorn

Two more tales that capture living and loving
beneath the Big Sky.

JUST PRETENDING by Myrna Mackenzie

FBI Agent David Hannon's plans for a quiet vacation
were overturned by a murder investigation—and by
officer Gretchen Neal!

STORMING WHITEHORN by Christine Scott

Native American Storm Hunter's return to Whitehorn
sent tremors through the town—and shock waves of
desire through Jasmine Kincaid Monroe....

Silhouette®

Where love comes alive™